The Dead Do Not Praise

The Dead Do Not Praise

Pauline Bell

St. Martin's Press
New York

Library of Congress Cataloging-in-Publication Data

Bell, Pauline.
　　The dead do not praise / Pauline Bell.
　　　　p.　cm.
　　"A Thomas Dunne book."
　　ISBN 0-312-09780-8
　　1. Police—England—Fiction.　I. Title.
　　PR6052.E443D4　1993
　　823'.914—dc20　　　　　　　　　　93-29086
　　　　　　　　　　　　　　　　　　　CIP

First published in Great Britain by Macmillan London Limited.

First U.S. Edition: December 1993
10　9　8　7　6　5　4　3　2　1

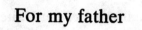
For my father

With grateful thanks to Peter Heaton and Lesley Lord
who answered countless questions.

Prologue

Not realising that this final Wednesday of September was to be the last day of her life, Sarah Bland, headmistress of Heath Lees High School, cut it shorter by sleeping through her bedside alarm. She was, therefore, for once, in no position to offer her tart greeting to the several members of her staff whose lateness was habitual.

If she had asked him, Kevin White would have explained that he gave his wife a lift to work each morning and that he atoned for his last-minute arrival by often being the last member of staff to leave at night. This morning he sighed as he watched Chris unlock 'Baby Bunting', knowing that she would spend her day there selling baby clothes to pregnant girls and new mothers whilst, with mounting impatience, she awaited signs of her own incipient motherhood. And, from what the latest tests revealed, it looked as though she would wait in vain.

Continuing his journey to school, White swung into Moorside Rise. At the point near the top, where the pavements approached each other in a narrow bottle-neck, a corporation dust-cart was parked. White changed gear, cursing the lack of common sense and good manners that allowed its driver to leave it there, and offered a prayer that his aged Mini would manage a hill start when the obstruction removed itself. The antics of his geriatric conveyance were a perpetual source of delight to his pupils, but he was not in the mood, this morning, to provide entertainment for the motley selection of them that was wending its way past him up the hill. He got his hand-brake to lock at the second

7

attempt, then he passed the time composing a letter of complaint to the council, pouring contempt on the mental capacities of its refuse collectors and its Highways Department, whilst the dust-cart, with much whirring of its internal mechanism, insolently raised its hind quarters to redistribute its load.

Running out of scornful invective, White abandoned his imaginary letter and turned his thoughts to the day ahead. The strengthening sun had almost dried the roads but rain had fallen heavily in the night. If it could be managed, he ought to keep the lads off that match pitch today. It would do the fourth-years good to put in a session of cross-country training, anyway. He'd better check the pitch before first lesson and see how quickly it was draining.

A couple of toddlers, open-mouthed and runny-nosed, emerged from a house further up the hill to watch the dust-cart right itself. Amused, White watched them as they supervised the transferring of their own dustbin to a trolley and trotted after it to oversee its emptying and witness its safe return to the stone slab outside their back door. A young woman followed them out. She was clad in slippers and a shabby housecoat but her make-up might have graced a gala night at the opera. Under spiky lashes, she peered up the street and located her offspring. Pausing to add the stub of her cigarette to the rest of the litter in the garden, she roughly hauled the infants back into the house, tossing her bleached head as she slammed the door.

White's fingers tightened on the wheel. What right had a woman like that to produce a houseful of children whilst he and Chris, with the nursery planned and budgeted for, waited and waited and nothing happened? Through the windscreen mirror he was surprised to see Meg Rivers draw up behind him and raised his hand in salute. Now he would have the forthright domestic science mistress to share with him Miss Bland's disapproval.

Mrs Rivers acknowledged his greeting, then looked over her shoulder to check that the various containers on the back seat were still in place with their contents intact. She listed, mentally, the ingredients for the dishes she intended to demonstrate in the first two periods. She was angry with herself for forgetting the gelatine. It wasn't like her to be inefficient and Brendan knew it. He probably thought she'd left it behind on purpose to give her an excuse to check up on him. She smiled, in spite of herself, remembering him at the telephone, soberly garbed for his business day, meticulously smoothing his hair and straightening his tie, as though this latest object of his affections could see him as he spoke to her.

Bringing her mind back to her day's work in the housecraft department, she tried to decide which of her demonstration dishes would be most suitable for their evening meal and realised that she would have to absent herself from morning assembly if she were to have everything set up ready for when the upper sixth arrived. In her wing mirror she noticed the biology mistress's yellow Strada join the queue of cars in Moorside Rise.

To reach it, Glenys Freebourne had had to drive past her mother's house at the corner. She had seen the curtain twitch and knew that her own last-minute scurry to work had been noted, along with the fine detail of every other event that had occurred that morning in view of that particular window. She had meant to be at least twenty minutes earlier but Neville had been extra difficult this morning. She wished for the hundredth time that he attended a different school. She might cope better with him at home if he hadn't the opportunity to embarrass her in front of her colleagues, all day, with his sulky lack of co-operation. Of course it wasn't really Nev's fault. A lot was expected of staff children by the rest of the staff, whilst, at the same time, they were open to suspicion and teasing from fellow pupils who thought they might tell tales or be given preferential treatment. Still holding her protesting vehicle on the clutch, she sighed deeply and pushed a strand of hair behind her ear. There wouldn't be time, now, to attend to the bees before school. She'd

9

have to do it during assembly. Miss Bland wasn't going to be pleased about that.

At last the dust-cart seemed to have swallowed up the offerings of Moorside Rise and be ready to depart. It made stuttering progress towards the brow of the hill, and the following train of cars, all with indicators announcing their intention, turned right into the school entrance beyond. To his relief, Kevin White's car obligingly restarted for this final stage of its journey.

They were all parked in a neat row by the time Julian Frayn appeared, his house, situated just opposite the school, facilitating such a tardy arrival. His eyes were alight from the battle he had just concluded with his wife. Thank the Lord he had married Kate and not some sensitive plant who burst into tears at the least criticism. Kate had defended herself with intelligence and vigour, and, looking about him, he was not sure that his own case was entirely sound. The paint on the gate was peeling and cracked and the lawn had ragged edges. Remembering the responsibility he had undertaken for the outside of the property, he decided that further comment today on the state of the kitchen was, perhaps, unwise, maybe even unfair.

He shrugged, then grinned at a scurrying, almost late sixth-former who, nevertheless, had the courtesy to stand back and allow his English master to precede him through the entrance to the foyer.

'In a hurry, Redfearn?'

'Yes, sir, I'm supposed to be at a meeting in the common room before registration.'

'Something important?'

The youth shrugged. 'Not really, sir. It's about raising funds for a new record player. I won't be much use to them; I'm not a financial genius.'

Remembering the lad's three attempts to obtain O-level maths, Frayn nodded. 'They'll probably do better without you. Tell them I kept you. Shall I see you at the lunch-time auditions today?'

The boy's face lit up. 'Definitely, sir. The whole A-level group's coming.'

'Do you think we'll be able to cast the set play from the people who turn up?'

'Oh, I think so, sir.' He frowned and went on more hesitantly, 'I heard someone say, sir, that Miss Bland doesn't think *A Winter's Tale* is very suitable for a school play. Shall we be allowed to do it? Is she objecting because it's about someone committing adultery?'

Frayn scowled. 'I thought you'd studied this play. Hermione doesn't commit adultery; Leontes only thinks she has. Anyhow, it's the only play I'm prepared to produce. I can't see how it can be right to study a play but wrong to stage it.' Frayn remembered his intention of tackling the head later in the day but was not so unprofessional as to elaborate on the subject even to this mature boy. 'What do you think of it?' he asked, veering away from the more dangerous topic.

'It's not a bad play, sir. I can see, now, why you made us read *Othello* as well, with both of them being about jealous husbands. Most of us think *Othello* is more of a tragedy.'

'Why's that?'

'Well, Othello was a good and great bloke. He only got jealous about his wife because Iago put the idea in his mind, so you feel more sorry for him. We all think that, except Val.'

'And what does Valerie think?'

'She says *A Winter's Tale* is a better play. She says people are either jealous or they're not and Leontes was. And she says people who're not, like Othello, never would be, even if Iago tried to make them.'

'A few exercises in clarity of expression wouldn't go amiss, but I take Valerie's point.' Frayn glanced at his watch. 'I must go. And you'd better get upstairs, Redfearn. I expect you'll find they've volunteered you for all the money-raising tasks that no one else would take on.'

Dismissing the boy, he hurried towards the staff room, pausing to sweep up a pile of exercise books from the large

11

pigeon-hole with his name over it in the row by the door. Tucking them under his arm, he went in and made his way to his customary place at one of the tables. Settling to mark them, he became absorbed into the general scene of sordid but systematised untidiness. A heap of books beside him threatened to collapse but didn't, even when he extracted a volume from near the bottom of the pile. Flicking through it, he checked a reference, then, turning back to the top exercise book, made a detailed marginal comment in red fountain-pen ink.

Meg Rivers, detaching herself from the bustle of activity round the urn, carried two cups of tea across the room and placed one beside him. He glanced up and smiled his thanks. 'A rush job.' he explained. 'I meant to dispose of these after the staff meeting last night but it went on so long. They're only getting a flick and tick.'

She pulled a face at him. 'Don't be so affected, Julian. You're correcting them with your usual meticulous attention, and, I suspect, adding the caustic but amusing remarks that your classes have learned to enjoy or dread according to how well they manage to please you.'

The staff room telephone rang. Rising from her armchair to answer it, Mrs Rivers observed, through the window, her headmistress's belated arrival. Miss Bland parked her car in its usual place which no one had dared appropriate, and strode off towards her own quarters, failing to greet, or even to notice, the young art mistress who almost collided with her. Arriving by the track leading up from the housing estate which sprawled down the hillside below the school, Sue Rogers was glad to have her tardiness ignored. She waited as a venerable and beautifully cared-for Morris 1000 entered the car park. From it, Penny Stafford of the history department emerged, scowling at the sunlight and holding a hand to her head. Meg watched as, supported by a sympathetic Sue, Miss Stafford stumbled into the building. Then she offered a last soothing word to the over-protective parent on the other end of the line, replaced the receiver and sighed.

Frayn, his flicking and ticking completed, followed the

12

direction of her gaze and chuckled. 'The morning's to be enlivened by a dying duck act from our Penny, I see. Bear up, Meg, it's all in a day's work.'

They were distracted from Miss Stafford's sufferings by a lurid oath from over by the pigeon-holes from which Kevin White had just removed a letter. He read it to the end, then crushed the sheet angrily, hurling it into the wastepaper-basket. 'Someone's going to do that old bat in before long,' he declared with considerable venom. 'If I were her, I wouldn't sit with my back to the door and that stupid, leering cat on the desk. It's too handy a weapon!' The feminine pronoun and the reference to the cat ornament identified the object of his displeasure as Miss Bland.

The deputy headmaster, breathless and perspiring, entered as the prophecy was uttered. 'What's she done now?'

White's kick sent the waste-bin spinning into the middle of the floor. 'It's what she hasn't done! Every other head of PE in Cloughton is going on a weekly course next term and it looked like tackling a few problems that have been rearing their ugly heads in this place for a while.'

'And she won't recommend it?' Shrugging sympathetically and leaving his own department to console him, Maynard turned to Frayn as he unzipped his tracksuit top and wiped the sweat from his forehead with the tea-cloth from the draining board. 'Pour me some tea, Julian. I got ten miles in this morning but I've only ten minutes to shower before assembly.'

'You're the sort that gets masochists a bad name,' Frayn told him as he complied with the request. In the chorus of titters that followed this sally, Maynard grabbed his cup and departed.

Meg Rivers picked up the ill-used tea-cloth from where Maynard had dropped it and consigned it to the laundry. She looked with distaste at the slimy wooden draining board and began to scrub it with hot, soapy water.

Further conversation was made impossible by fifteen seconds of mind-battering jangling from the electric bell over the door. It was the signal for form tutors to grab a register

13

from the appropriate table and depart to mark present such pupils as awaited them in their form rooms. They did so with the customary grumbles, casting envious glances at their few favoured colleagues who were excused this menial duty for the current year. Sue Rogers, who should have belonged to this privileged company, took a yellow-backed register and prepared to depart.

Kevin White, who was excused too, looked up. 'Who's absent?' he enquired.

'No one as far as I know, but,' Sue indicated Miss Stafford, slumped in a chair, an empty coffee cup beside her, 'Penny's got a migraine so I'm dealing with her lot for her.' She departed, and, with her, all sympathy for the recumbent Penny.

'I've got the bees to see to and Meg's got a demonstration to set up.' Having absolved herself and her colleague from any obligation to minister to the invalid, Glenys Freebourne went out. Kevin White, feeling that his contempt for an indisputable malingerer needed no excuse, turned his back on her and poured himself more tea.

Ten minutes later, their ears were once more assaulted by the bell and a thunderous, echoing pounding in the corridor indicated that the school was reporting to the hall for its morning devotions. Soon, the pounding was partially overpowered by a brisk organ voluntary, competently if insensitively executed. It served its purpose of drowning the sounds of the less than reverent preliminaries to the school's daily act of worship.

It seemed to White, after a while, that the music was more than usually protracted. To Geoff Maynard, standing with his two colleagues on the hall platform, a sea of faces looking expectantly towards him, it seemed much more so. Reaching the end of a cadence, the organist looked towards him and received a nod to continue playing. The school fidgeted. Knowing that talking in assembly was followed by dire penalties its members commented to each other with ventriloquial skill. Maynard consulted his watch and then his fellow deputies about the headmistress's non-appearance to

14

conduct the proceedings. 'What's keeping her? She might have let us know.'

'Shall I go and see?'

Brenda Viner turned down the third deputy's offer. 'It'll take too long, Roger. We'd better go ahead without her. You take the service, Geoff, whilst I check the notice book.'

Maynard stepped to the front of the platform and attention switched back to him. He raised his hymn book and looked towards the organ. Rightly interpreting the gesture, the music master signalled the hymn number with a display of fingers, and, after it was announced, played it at a lively pace, as though to make up for lost time. The pupils sang lustily, knowing the painful consequences of what their musical director referred to as 'faint praise'.

Under cover of the hymn, Maynard flicked through the Bible on the lectern, hoping to find a reasonably appropriate portion of scripture before the sixth and final verse was completed. He lighted upon Psalm 115 and his measured and dignified delivery of it revealed no trace of his irritation. A choral rendering of the Lord's Prayer followed and the platform party was satisfied that the law had been well and truly complied with.

Maynard waited until Mrs Viner had begun on the day's allocation of notices and slipped out on a burst of applause for a major soccer victory. He walked past the staff room and cloakrooms, then along a corridor lined with classrooms, towards the administration corridor which contained the school office and the head's study. First, he poked his head round the office door, where the head's secretary was applying cleaning fluid to a biro stain on the pocket of a man's tweed jacket.

'Where's Her Majesty?' he enquired.

Mrs Weston dabbed more fluid on the pocket and looked up. 'Still in assembly, I suppose. Can I do anything?'

'She didn't come to assembly! Brenda and I did it between us.'

Mrs Weston shrugged and filled the pocket with a paper

15

towel to absorb the now liquefied stain. 'I've been dupli-cating,' she explained, 'so if something important turned up she obviously didn't bother to interrupt me.'

Maynard was annoyed. 'That's all very well but she should have let us know to take assembly for her. I wonder how long she'll be tied up.' Receiving no answer to his tap on the communicating door, Maynard opened it and looked into the head's room. At first glance, all appeared to be as usual. Miss Bland was seated at her desk, head bent closely over it. But she was occupied by no urgent school business, detained by no visitor or important telephone call. Mrs Weston, close on Maynard's heels, pushed past him and entered the room in front of him. As they both moved forward they realised that the headmistress had been prevented from leading the school's morning worship by an assortment of injuries to the face and head, and that the combination of them had been fatal.

Chapter 1

'The dead do not praise!' Maynard announced and gave a half hysterical bark of laughter. 'I've just read it in what should have been her assembly.' Ignoring Carol Weston's look of astonishment he backed to the doorway again, struggling to subdue his nausea. Inside his head he encouraged himself. At least he didn't have to touch the body, to assist with first aid. Miss Bland was undoubtedly dead. He didn't even have to go any further into the room. In fact, to do so would be unwise, against established police procedure. He'd better get on to the police at once, after he'd attended to Carol. He ought to get her a chair and a glass of water. He began to see to it, trying to still his shaking hands and uncomfortably aware that hers would be steady.

She brushed him aside, impatiently, scornful of his discomposure. 'I'll ring the police,' she offered, passing him with a swish of elegant skirt and going to the telephone on the desk in her own office. With her finger in the dial, she circled it rapidly, her eyes on Maynard's tormented face. His eyes were closed, the thick black lashes sweeping ashen cheeks as he fought waves of faintness. He both needed and resented her initiative; she was triumphantly aware of both his need and his resentment.

Her contempt provoked an anger which helped him master his distress. He drew a deep breath, and, when he spoke, though his voice still shook, he was beginning to gain command of himself. 'Thanks. You do that. We'd better not go in there again. In fact, I'll make sure no one does.' He took a substantial bunch of keys from his jacket pocket and locked the door between the office and the head's study. Then he went out to lock the one that opened into the corridor. Out of the secretary's view, he leaned against the wall, pressing his forehead against the cold painted plaster and feeling the prick of perspiration across his shoulder blades. When he returned to the office, Mrs Weston had finished her call to the police.

'We'd better let school proceed normally until someone arrives.' Maynard felt a further surge of restorative anger as she considered his remark before nodding her consent. He'd intended to give an instruction, not ask her advice. He cursed his apologetic manner but couldn't yet find it in himself to dominate her. 'We must at least let Brenda and Roger know,' he continued, rapidly, before she could take the lead again. 'Try the staff room. They probably haven't gone about their business yet. Don't tell them anything over the phone. Just ask them to come here.'

Detective Constable Benedict Mitchell proceeded in the mellow sunshine past his old school. Seen from the opposite side of the road, it had margins of trees at each side of it, which overhung the dirty, yellow sandstone wall that had bordered the field for more years than the school had been standing in it. The main block of more recently hewn and cleaner sandstone, punctuated by areas of glass, stood silent, giving no sign of life within. Glancing at his watch, and casting his mind back a little, Mitchell worked out that first lesson would be under way.

He spared a thought for those who were suffering it and smiled to himself. He had been a spirited and resourceful but not exemplary pupil. He had not always seen eye to eye with his mentors, several of whom had raised their eyebrows when he had been welcomed into the ranks of the local force. It had amused him to be the officer sent to deal with one of the school's occasional requests for police assistance and to read, in the faces of the school's hierarchy, the opinion that for him to run to earth the miscreant they were pursuing was less than justice.

18

Faint cries reached him from the football pitches on the other side of the buildings and, dismissing a wave of regret for the passing of his games lessons at least, he walked on down the hill, pausing to take note of the number of a disreputable-looking car which had been parked now for some forty-eight hours dangerously near the junction of Lees Ridge and Moorside Rise. Scoring a thick line under this latest entry, Mitchell tucked his notebook into his pocket.

When the radio, clipped to his jacket, bleeped, he felt somewhat aggrieved. The previous evening, the jeweller in the town precinct had been relieved of the centrepiece of his new window display. Mitchell had his ideas about the perpetrator of this theft. The mother of his suspect was the neighbour of his old aunt on the estate opposite the school. As the local boy, he had managed to convince Inspector Browne that he could persuade both ladies to confide in him. He'd better not be having second thoughts now.

His resentment soon turned to excitement as he absorbed the news that his crackling radio imparted. Just fancy! Somebody had done for the old bird. He supposed, on reflection, that as headmistresses went, she was a fairly young bird. Not a popular one though. When Browne wanted to know who had a sufficient grudge against her, he would come up with more answers than he'd bargained for.

Quickly retracing his steps, he concentrated on reaching the school as soon as possible. He well realised that he would be exercising his authority there for only as long as it took his superior officers to disengage themselves from their high-powered but nevertheless routine tasks. If he acquitted himself well it could only improve his recommendation for accelerated promotion.

Having resigned himself to slow and steady progress in his chosen career – not a policy he had favoured whilst at school – he had been enthusiastic about the special course Inspector Browne had told him about. Under Miss Bland's regime, Mitchell had regarded lessons as a battle of wits between himself and his instructor. In the staff room his attempts to halt the progress of his own studies and those

19

of his compeers had been discussed more often than his academic and social potential. The stringent discipline of the force had brought out the best in him and the twelve months he had spent in Sergeant Tuckey's section had convinced Inspector Browne that he had the makings of an excellent senior detective. To aim for the rank of Inspector by the fifth year of service was ambitious. To vie for one of sixty places offered to ten thousand or more constables seemed more so. His application would have amused most of his former teachers, though not, perhaps, Mr Frayn or Mr Maynard. He must use this big chance. Not only was he the nearest officer to the incident but he also had an intimate knowledge of its location which could only be a great advantage.

His radio bleeped again as he hurried through the main gate and, amidst more crackling and hissing, informed him that Dr Stocks was on his way. Mitchell was glad to hear it. Stocks was an experienced police surgeon who could offer him plenty of hints about the correct form for the enquiry to take. He hoped the rest of the team would be a long time arriving. Dr Stocks was articulate and willing to instruct. Mitchell determined to listen carefully, note and remember.

He had reached the main gate so turned into the drive, noticing that the nameplate, bearing the legend ' ATH LE S IGH SCHOO ', had been vandalised again, the offenders undeterred by the education authority notice alongside it, forbidding 'unauthorised access, the playing of games or exercising of dogs', with the threat of prosecution. Mitchell knew that the dogs in this area exercised – and often fed – themselves, and that the games played on their property by the trespassers so addressed exceeded the powers of the council's imagination.

Coming closer to the building, Mitchell observed an L-plate and a recently made dent on the back of Mr Maynard's car, parked against the fence that bounded the dustbin area. He surmised that Maynard's middle daughter was now learning to drive and knew that, until the registration bell had rung, the fence had hidden a meeting of the smokers' club, of which, not too long ago, he had been a leading light. In the entrance to the foyer was a group of youngsters. They looked like second- or third- years and were obviously waiting for a member of staff to collect them. Their subdued conversation suggested imminent supervision and their relaxed stance showed they were not truants from a lesson. Mitchell grinned at the currently fashionable efforts they had made to improve on the regulation maroon and grey. Pop stars' faces grimaced from badges on their lapels. Their ties were knotted at the wrong end, the broad flaps tucked inside their shirts and the thin tails hanging, miserably, down in front. Most of the boys as well as the girls sported several earrings. The children brightened at the sight of him and began to speculate with some animation on the reason for his presence. Keeping out of hailing distance, he passed what appeared to be the main entrance, knowing that it had been superseded when the new block was built which now contained the administration corridor with the school office and the head's study.

Maynard, watching through the office window for the arrival of the police, saw Mitchell with a sinking heart. The nightmare was going to be aggravated. Now he must proceed under the mocking gaze not only of the head's supercilious secretary but of this past pupil. He didn't dislike Mitchell; he could see much good in the boy but the school had not even begun to tap his potential, and Mitchell would be sufficiently intelligent to realise it and judge them. He walked out into the corridor and through the fire doors to meet him.

Mitchell noticed his pallor and smiled sympathetically. 'Well, this is a turn-up, sir,' he greeted him.

'It's certainly that, Benny.' Maynard let the fire doors swing shut. 'Do I call you Detective Constable Mitchell, now?'

'I shouldn't bother about it, sir. We've plenty else to think about.' He fished out his pencil and began his logging of the case by noting his own arrival. 'Now, sir, if you could give me the main facts whilst we're waiting for the police surgeon to get here.'

Maynard hesitated. 'Don't you want to see the body first?'

Mitchell considered. 'Frankly, I don't know what I should do first, sir. It's my first murder.'

'Well, it's my first, too. I think you should certainly inspect it briefly. I'll tell you what. We'll open the door and you can look in. Then, if you should have examined the corpse – and there's no doubt that it is one – you have done. And if you should have left it to your superiors you won't have done any harm.' Maynard was gaining confidence by the minute. He went to carry out his suggestion, wrapping his hand in his still-clean handkerchief and moving towards the door that led to Miss Bland's room from the corridor. Mitchell nodded approval of the handkerchief but put out his hand for it and the enormous bunch of keys that Maynard pulled from his bulging pocket. He couldn't have suspects smudging fingerprints whilst he looked on. He paused for a moment, enjoying this novel view of his erstwhile deputy headmaster, then carefully unlocked the door and turned the handle himself.

'Don't open the office door,' Maynard's voice said from behind him. 'We don't want to upset Mrs Weston again.'

Mitchell grinned. The bossy old cow would be much more upset if she thought any part of the affair was being conducted without her. He heard Mrs Viner's voice through the connecting door and knew who was keeping the secretary out of the way.

Maynard stood in the doorway and looked out of the window, thankful to find that his stomach could cope with this. Mitchell regarded the body with frank curiosity. This dumpy woman who appeared to have fallen asleep over her work seemed to have little connection with the headmistress who had harassed his existence for his last two years at school. There was a ragged, split wound across the right side of her brow but the thick, springy hair, clotted now with blood, prevented the full extent of the injuries being realised without closer examination. Carefully, he reached over and satisfied himself that there was no pulse. Touching nothing else, he scrutinised the scene.

He was surprised to find himself quite calm, his brain systematically assimilating his observations. The skull seemed to have been damaged in several places. Blood had sprayed finely from the lacerations, patterning the objects on the desk and the wall above it. The head rested on the wrist of the right arm bent beneath it and the blood had run down to the under surfaces. Mitchell, looking round for a weapon, gave consideration to the model cat that stood beside Miss Bland's right elbow. He thought it might well have done the damage, except that it seemed clean. As far as he could see, only its white base was marked by the blood which had trickled over the arm towards it.

He bent nearer to examine more closely the fine crimson spotting that covered the papers on the desk. In the middle was a small, clean, oblong patch of white. Something had been removed from the desk after the killing.

Mitchell turned round and went back to the corridor. Lowering himself into the nearest of the three chairs that stood against the wall, he recorded his findings.

'I'd like to keep your keys, sir.'

Maynard reached over and selected for Mitchell the master key, letting the others hang from it. The young constable relocked the study door and they entered the office from the corridor. There he found the other two deputies sitting on upright chairs whilst Carol Weston busied herself with a coffee percolator over by the window. She flashed a smile at the two of them. 'Finished your holy huddle, have you? I take it you won't mind if we all have some coffee, Dominic.'

Indicating permission, Mitchell went back to the corridor. Maynard, stung to retaliation said, tartly, 'If you want to establish a rapport with the local constabulary, I suggest you get their names right. It's Benedict. And I shouldn't take anything too much for granted at the moment.'

She waved an airy hand. 'I knew it was one of those fancy saints' names. You often find them bestowed on the worst of the sinners.' She returned to the production of her usual superb coffee, and Maynard, who needed it most, subsided and drank gratefully.

23

In the corridor, Mitchell's agonising over what he should do next was cut short by the arrival of Dr Stocks, and a moment later the door opened again to admit Detective Constable Richard Dean. Briefly, Mitchell put the two new arrivals in the picture and, seeing the young constable's hesitation, Stocks took charge. 'I suggest you listen in to the quartet in the office, Dean. Grill them a bit, before they have time to concoct any fairy stories. Mitchell here can be skivvy for me.'

Mitchell's face lit up and, producing Maynard's keys, he let the two of them into the study again. The police surgeon's job was soon dealt with. 'I can pronounce death without any difficulty. How did you check?'

'I couldn't feel any pulse, sir.'

Stocks nodded. 'We'll double check with a stethoscope. I think I can slip it on to the chest without disturbing things too much if I approach from the left.' His hands busied themselves about Miss Bland's neckline.

Satisfied that life was extinct and that murder had been committed, Stocks confirmed that it would be in order for Mitchell to summon the Home Office pathologist without waiting for the arrival of his superiors. Mitchell used the office telephone to do so, then, leaving Dean to continue his interrogation, returned to watch Dr Stocks stowing away his stethoscope.

'I suppose, sir,' he began, hopefully, 'it wouldn't be possible . . . ?'

'For me to put in a word for you with Dr Ledgard? As a matter of fact I'd like a quick word with him before I go. All right, I'll try to convince him that watching him do his stuff with this particular corpse will make all the difference to your acceptance on this course you've set your heart on.'

Mitchell thanked him effusively and his delight when Ledgard proved amenable to this scheme made Stocks feel well repaid for his trouble.

Mitchell had been intimidated on his first acquaintance with the tall, gaunt pathologist. The high colour in the hollow cheeks and the grizzled auburn hair had suggested a choleric temperament and the blue eyes had seemed to smile frostily. Over a hit and run incident where they had fleetingly worked together, he had learned that the impatience and unfriendliness had been in his own mind, invented by his nervousness. Now he greeted the doctor with a bashful enthusiasm, noting that his barber had done an even more drastic job than usual and marvelling that so fleshless a physique had so little difficulty in heaving around the bulging case of equipment.

Mitchell was scrutinised in his turn. From their previous conversations Ledgard was aware of Mitchell's ambitions and anxious to encourage them. He liked the stocky, open-faced youngster and was sure he had the qualities he needed to turn his pretensions into achievements. He was hard-working when motivated and had already shown considerable physical courage.

They presented an incongruous picture, standing together, the young constable, broad-shouldered and bullet-headed and barely tall enough to be recruited, reaching just past the chin of his six-foot companion. They surveyed the body in silence for a moment before Ledgard began his quiet, meticulous examination, giving a commentary on his findings for Mitchell's benefit.

'I doubt if we'll need medical evidence to establish the time of death. Presumably her secretary saw her arrive and doubtless several other people did too. Dean will soon find out what time the body was discovered and that will probably fix the time more accurately than I can. The blood's congealing except where it's in pools. The body temperature is still almost normal but this room is very warm. I'd say it happened about an hour ago. Now then, Mitchell, what about cause of death? Presumably you'd had a quick look before I arrived. What theories have you got to propound?'

'Multiple wounds to the head and temple, sir.'

'Yes,' Ledgard encouraged him.

'By a blunt instrument?' Mitchell went on.

'Good. How do you know that?'

25

'Because they aren't good deep cuts, sir. It's more as if the skin split because it was crushed and stretched.'

'Excellent. What about a weapon?'

'Could it be the cat, sir?'

'Why?'

'Well, it's about the right shape and easy to grab hold of and it's handy. It can't be, though.'

'Why not?'

'It's not bloodstained.'

'I think it is a little. Look at the back of its head. But I agree, it's not very messy. You've already explained that, though.'

Mitchell frowned as he thought back but failed to take Ledgard's point.

The doctor took pity on him. 'You told me that a blow from a blunt instrument causes crushing of the skin. It also crushes the blood vessels, temporarily. Probably several seconds elapsed before bleeding commenced and our customer seems to have been seeing how many different targets he could hit. He hasn't made repeated blows in one place. If each one had a new location, we wouldn't find much staining of the weapon.'

Mitchell filed away this information, then raised another point. 'You said "he", sir. Would it need a man's strength?'

Ledgard grinned. 'I used the pronoun carelessly. What do you think?'

'I think anyone could have done it, sir, even a pupil.'

'And I think I agree with you. Left- or right-handed? Any other ideas?'

'It wouldn't need to be anybody tall, sir. Miss Bland was sitting down. I think it would have to be a right-handed person.'

'I'll endorse that, too.' He paused as he heard voices outside, some of which he recognised. 'Your bosses are arriving, Mitchell. I think this twosome is about to be interrupted. The rest of your morning is likely to be a bit less interesting, I'm afraid.'

'There's one other thing, sir. Had you noticed this?'

Mitchell pointed to the clean, oblong shape on the blood-spattered desk.

'I had, Mitchell. You'd better report your observation of it to your betters.'

Not sharing Mitchell's familiarity with the geography of the school, Sergeant Hunter and Inspector Browne had come in by the old main entrance. Each of them had a child who was a pupil in the school and both were feeling, already, an unwonted personal anxiety about this case. Browne, whose daughter had reached the sixth form, had attended enough school functions to know that the assembly hall and staff room were on the corridor leading to the right, whilst the one going left led, past classrooms, to the dining-room. Since Virginia was hard-working and law-abiding he had never been summoned to discuss her work or behaviour in the privacy of the head's study and had had no reason, yet, to locate it. Hunter, whose eleven-year-old son was in the first year, was at a greater disadvantage.

They paused in the entrance, absorbing the atmosphere. Since the school was built into the hillside, the foyer was in a well with stairs leading up to balcony corridors. Below the balcony rail and beside the stairs stood two wooden troughs, planted with an assortment of ivies whose fight for existence was being swiftly subdued by warm gusts of dry air from the central heating ducts beneath them. In the corner, on a wooden plinth, stood a remarkable piece of sculpture in metal, the work, Browne knew, of one of his daughter's classmates. Its subject was a mystery to him, but, whatever had inspired it, the result was graceful and elegant. Beside it in a shelved, glass-fronted cabinet, several rows of sporting trophies were displayed, each adorned with a ribbon in a primary colour, denoting, presumably, the house that currently possessed it. Having done their best to make an attractive display on the corridor side of the foyer, the authorities had consigned to the opposite corner a collection of objects whose usefulness justified their unsightly appearance: a public telephone attached to the wall, a fire hose in

27

a recess and an ugly but serviceable-looking wheelchair.

Maynard's office was on the right of the main entrance, clearly labelled. Browne tapped, stuck his head round the door and blinked. He had not expected to find Maynard there, nor to find his room in such sordid chaos. A huge blackboard, filled with brightly coloured pegs, was propped on the window-sill, presumably the current timetable waiting to be dismantled. Piles of exercise books, files and papers covered every available surface, overflowing from wire baskets. On top of some of these, on the desk, had been flung a heap of damp running gear, a black track suit and a vest and pair of shorts in a startling green.

Coming back into the foyer, he found Hunter in conversation with a small boy who was importantly giving directions to Miss Bland's room. Thanking him gravely, Hunter allowed the child to continue to the staff room with his request for more chalk and the two policemen made for the scene of the crime. As they passed the dining-room, they smelled, not the half-anticipated school boiled cabbage but an appetising aroma of herbs and onions, which was superseded as they pushed open the fire doors by the offensive toxic reek of duplicating fluid. Browne knocked on the office door and opened it just as Ledgard and Mitchell emerged from the study. Suddenly the corridor was full of people. The group of academics and the group of policemen stood for a moment, making a swift appraisal of each other. Beside Hunter, even Ledgard seemed to be only of average height and the Inspector was dwarfed. Nevertheless, Browne had about him an air of command that left no doubt which was the senior officer.

Maynard realised that the detectives had entered the school by the old main door and he greeted Browne apologetically. 'I'm sorry you were misled and probably had to ask your way. We had a notice put up directing visitors round but, of course, the vandals had their own uses for it and it disappeared.'

Browne wondered whether his bleak expression was

caused by the school's inability to quell its unruly element or the deficiencies of the police who had failed to do it for them. He shook hands with Maynard. 'We haven't time to chase them today. If we can just have a look at things, we'll get under way.' Maynard nodded and indicated the head's door.

Before entering the study, Browne turned to the two constables who were hanging back against the wall. 'Till we get reinforcements, I shall need you two to relieve us of the press and doubtless a posse of curious youngsters. Dean, you'd better look after these fire doors and prevent access from the dining-room area.' He turned to the three teachers. 'Where does the other end of this corridor lead?'

'To a cloakroom and an outside door to the playing field.' Brenda Viner addressed him for the first time.

Browne nodded. 'That's yours, then, Mitchell. You can admire the moorland view and be inhospitable to anyone from outside who comes visiting.' Noticing the constable's crestfallen expression, he sharpened his tone. 'The fact that I'm recommending you for accelerated promotion, Mitchell, doesn't let you out of your share of menial tasks.'

Mitchell acknowledged this with a muttered, 'Sir.'

Dean self-righteously stationed himself where he could fulfil his duties without being too much in evidence to children who might have legitimate occasion to wander the bottom corridor.

Mitchell handed over a notebook to the inspector. 'I'd started a log, sir.' Browne accepted it without comment and Mitchell departed up the corridor. Closing the door behind him, he philosophically regarded the rising hillside, its bald patches, scrubbed by the wind, looking shabbier than usual in this morning's unkind sunlight. He grinned to himself as he savoured Ledgard's parting wink.

The party indoors was less happy. Maynard was steeling himself to deal with his newly acquired secretary, his fellow deputies, temporarily, at least, his underlings, the chairman

29

of the governors and the education office. Browne and Hunter were even more anxious than usual to get their enquiries under way. There was a murderer at large, probably in this very building where their daughter and son, respectively, were innocently pursuing their studies.

Chapter 2

As a school parent, Browne was familiar with Maynard in his official capacity. He had liked his friendly and unassuming but authoritative manner and was surprised now to see how tenuous a grip he had on himself. The right hand shifted objects unnecessarily about the office desk whilst the left rumpled the back of the unruly black hair. Browne had observed this habit in nervous small boys but most of them grew out of it in their teens. Perhaps they smoked instead. Maynard didn't. He did, however, demonstrate a wish to be co-operative.

'I – er suppose you'll want some sort of base to work from, Inspector. I'm not sure that my office would be suitable.'

Remembering it, Browne heartily agreed but he demurred tactfully. 'It's rather too far away from the scene, Mr Maynard. I'm afraid we're going to have to use this area. Was that the dining-room I passed on the left as I came in?'

All four of them affirmed it.

'Perhaps, when we've had a brief word, you could all wait in there.'

Maynard agreed listlessly, Blythe and Mrs Viner resignedly. Mrs Weston opened her mouth to say that it wasn't convenient at all but was quelled by the look with which Browne had silenced more intimidating personalities than hers.

He settled himself in Mrs Weston's chair and his manner became businesslike. 'Obviously, the most important thing

I want to know at this moment is when and by whom Miss Bland was last seen alive.'

Mrs Weston, aggrieved by Browne's snub and resentful of his usurpation of her chair, nevertheless could not resist the opportunity to take the floor. 'She overslept this morning,' she offered. 'She didn't arrive at school until nearly twenty to nine. I made coffee – I already had the kettle boiling – and I took her cup in to her before the registration bell rang. I drank mine in here but the door was ajar and I could hear her taking off her things and getting herself organised. I think she started writing a letter. After the bell rang, Julian came in and I went off to do some duplicating for him. I thought Miss Bland had gone to assembly when I'd finished so I got on in here.'

Browne thanked her for this unsolicited but useful information. 'Did anyone else see her after the registration bell? What time does it go?'

'Eight fifty.' Brenda Viner spoke for the second time and Browne wondered how much longer Roger Blythe would remain silent. 'Normally, Miss Bland goes to Geoff's room during registration. Roger and I meet there too for a swap of information and to make last-minute arrangements before the day starts. We three met there as usual.'

'Brenda had seen the head arrive late and in a hurry,' Maynard put in, 'so we weren't surprised when she didn't come across.' His manner was becoming more relaxed and he gave Browne a ghost of the friendly grin that had charmed many irate parents. 'No one had been reported absent – on the staff, I mean – and nothing untoward was scheduled, no trips out or visiting speakers and so on, so I sent Brenda and Roger off for a quick coffee. I think I said it was going to be the only straightforward day this week so we didn't need a meeting.' The grin broke through in earnest until he remembered it was inappropriate and the bleak look resettled.

Browne turned back to Mrs Weston. 'Who's Julian?'

'Mr Frayn. He's in the English department and head of sixth form.'

Browne nodded and Hunter, now seated on an upright chair behind him, scribbled in his own shorthand.

'And did Mr Frayn visit Miss Bland?'

'No, he came out of the office with me and went off towards the staff room. He left his jacket behind,' she added, inconsequentially. 'His biro had leaked all over the pocket. I've fixed it, though.' She indicated, with her usual air of self-congratulation, the pristine pocket of the jacket in question, which still hung over the typing chair.

Hunter went on writing and his chief turned to Maynard again. 'What time was it when you and Mrs Weston discovered the body?'

Maynard re-rumpled his hair and deepened his frown. 'I'm not sure. Assembly's usually over at nine twenty but we were late starting and finishing. Then it takes a couple of minutes to walk along the bottom corridor from the hall. It was probably nine twenty-five, not less anyway.'

Browne heard the welcome sounds of reinforcements arriving. 'Just one last thing. What time does first lesson end?'

'Ten fifteen. Any time now.'

'Right. Mrs Weston, I want you to delay that bell. Let them all stay where they are for another minute or two. When it does ring, I want the whole school, pupils, staff, caretaker and secretary to go to the main hall, avoiding this corridor, of course. I'll send two or three men around with a message.'

'It would be more easily organised and less upsetting for the children if we four did it.'

So Roger Blythe hadn't taken a vow of silence. Browne nodded at him. 'I think I can allow that.'

Unbidden, Carol Weston had moved to a wall timetable and, running her finger along a line of it, had begun to make a list of which rooms were occupied during the current lesson.

'If you divide that list between three of you, I'd like some more information from Mr Maynard.' Browne waved him to a seat as the others set off obediently, then turned to his sergeant. 'Jerry, will you go with Mr Maynard and face the curious multitude? Let him speak to them first. You'd better tell them Miss Bland has met with a fatal accident. Some of them will have seen us arrive and they'll know it's more than a smashed window we're asking about.'

He glanced at the timetable Mrs Weston had referred to and the list of duties beside it, blessing the monotonously repeated school routine with its bells and schedules. Some of them may have been ignored or evaded but they made it abundantly clear where everyone should have been and when. He consulted Maynard about the normal procedure for registration and morning assembly.

Maynard took his left hand from the lock of hair it was twiddling and imprisoned it on his lap in his right. 'Miss Bland's instructions are for form teachers to go to their forms, stay with them during registration, accompany them to assembly and dismiss them from there. I suppose most of them do it most of the time.'

'Fair enough. Jerry, when Mr Maynard has broken the news to them, have a word, then send them all back to the rooms where they registered, staff included. Those staff who didn't have registers to mark are to stay in the hall and remember to keep them well apart from each other.'

Ignoring Maynard's questioning eyebrows, he dismissed both men and they set off down the corridor towards the hall. Alone for a few moments, Browne found his personal fear rising to the surface of his mind again. Where was Virginia now and who with? As if in answer to his question, the bell which Mrs Weston had reset began to ring and he knew his daughter would be on her way to the hall in company with several hundred other pupils. He recalled his mind to his own duties, went out to the corridor and entered the head's study from there to see what Ledgard had to tell him.

He found the pathologist packing his belongings back into their sectioned box and ready to make his preliminary report. Ledgard outlined concisely the evidence that supported his opinion that Miss Bland had been fatally struck with the model Egyptian cat on her desk by a right-handed

34

person of undetermined sex and size. 'I think she was sitting squarely, facing her desk with her back to the room, either unaware of her attacker's presence or ignoring it.' He slipped a pair of tweezers into the appropriate slot. 'The assailant was probably directly behind her and grabbed the weapon from the window side of the desk. She turned to her right to see what was happening and her right temple caught the first blow.' He explained to Browne why the weapon was only slightly bloodstained. 'Young Mitchell deduced a good deal of that – and was careful to point out that unspattered patch on the papers on the desk.'

Browne smiled. 'Bright lad, isn't he? Think he'll be able to take the hard time he's going to be given?'

Ledgard considered. 'He isn't afraid of hard work or physical danger. I think he'll do well.'

'I meant the hard time his colleagues will give him.' Browne handed the last of the intimidating instruments to be stowed away. 'The rank and file don't take kindly to the system. If he's elevated to sergeant's rank, experimentally, so to speak, he'll be working with resentful peers. It's half jealousy and half the quite justifiable objection that he'll lack their experience and therefore, possibly, their wisdom and judgment. Ah, well, we shall see.'

Both men looked up and through the window as car doors were heard slamming outside. 'Here come the SOCO boys. Let's hope we haven't queered their pitch for them.'

Going out into the corridor, he greeted Donaldson and Swann, shook hands with the Coroner's Officer who came in behind them and nodded to Constable Nigel Bellamy, who stood deferentially by the fire doors. Through them came, once again, the thunderous sound of footfalls, accompanied by shrill comment as several hundred pupils discussed their headmistress's demise. Inviting the Scenes of Crime Officers to be about their business, Browne passed through the fire doors with a smile for Dean who was still guarding them. Multitudes of children, displaying excitement rather than grief, jostled their way down the main corridor, disappearing round corners and up staircases.

A voice, raised in authority, thundered behind them, after which they proceeded with considerably more courtesy and less noise. This was the Maynard that Browne was familiar with, made easy by the unquestioning respect of his pupils. Catching his eye, the Inspector motioned him to follow him into the dining-hall. It was a large room full of hard surfaces. One wall consisted of floor-to-ceiling windows and, in spite of some autumn sunshine and areas of primrose yellow walls, it both looked and felt cold. Browne repressed a shiver and coveted the academic gown which Maynard drew more closely round him.

Sensing that some hospitality was due from him as acting headmaster, Maynard indicated tubular chairs with backrests and seats of moulded plastic in a particularly nasty shade of chocolate brown. Feeling slightly foolish, Browne seated himself at an octagonal table, the two separate halves of which were covered with garish laminated plastic in unmatching designs. He observed that two similar unmatching halves formed the next table. Maynard, who ate there every day, was perfectly at home.

'I take it you are now automatically in charge here,' Browne began.

Maynard nodded. 'I suppose so. If the head's absent, one of my duties is to deputise for her until her return. Whether I continue to do so for more than a few days depends on what the governors decide, although I don't see what else they can do until there's been time to advertise for a successor and go through all the rigmarole of choosing one.' He fixed his gaze on a three-tier trolley, used to collect and wheel away nauseating leftovers rejected by several hundred indulged and finicky juvenile appetites. Making a visible effort, he wrested the initiative from the Inspector. 'I realise I have to answer your questions but I really need to ask some first. Will school be allowed to remain in session? If not, there are arrangements to be made with the transport people, the school dinner to cancel and so on. And I must put the governors in the picture.'

He paused, and Browne registered the subdued sounds of

kitchen utensils being plied which came through the closed hatches at the far end of the room. He made up his mind quickly. 'You'll have to shut up shop for the rest of today, so you'd better cancel your meal, but don't arrange transport until we've decided how many people we need to detain to help with enquiries. We should be able to let most people go when we've checked all the group alibis.'

He got up and put his head round the door to give Constable Bellamy an appropriate message for the school cook, then returned to his incongruous seat.

Maynard looked puzzled. 'Group alibis?'

'We have Mrs Weston's evidence that Miss Bland was alive and well when the registration bell rang, so we can probably send home any form that remained as a unit from then till the end of assembly, together with its form teacher. Now it's time for my questions.'

Maynard nodded and braced himself, fixing his blue stare this time on an assortment of spare canvas chairs precariously stacked in a corner.

'Before we begin on "Where were you at the time . . . " perhaps you could give me some idea of the set-up here. How long ago was Miss Bland appointed?'

'It would have been five years at Christmas,' Maynard volunteered. 'She came from a school near Canterbury where she'd been first deputy.'

'And was she a good head?'

The left hand was rumpling the back hair again; the face wore a ferocious scowl.

'I'm not asking for a scrupulously objective assessment,' Browne assured him. 'I just want a general impression.'

'Well, she wasn't really headship material. She was self-conscious, prickly and awkward. But she did have her points. She had a very disciplined mind. She'd have made a good accountant or actuary. The timetable will never be constructed so efficiently again, or the school's finances so well managed.' The frown deepened as he endeavoured to be fair. 'She just couldn't cope with school when there were people in it.'

'That's rather a serious handicap.'

Maynard leaned forward, confidentially. 'As a matter of fact, whoever did this jumped the gun. She was seriously thinking of taking up a job with figures and getting out of this place.'

Browne took up the inference. 'You're assuming the killer worked or attended here, then? Surely it's pretty easy for an outsider to get in, isn't it?'

'Yes, but not for him to go unremarked. Kids are great observers and the staff keep an eye open because intruders usually mean trouble, truants from the school across the estate intent on vandalism, angry or anxious parents, our own old pupils. They're very conspicuous. Everyone knows them and knows they shouldn't be there.'

'Do you think, then, that Miss Bland was sufficiently "prickly" to make someone in school murderously angry?'

Maynard shrugged. 'I don't know. But in the present economic climate, a member of staff who found her insufferable would be trapped. It's very difficult, these days, to change jobs and move away.' He stopped speaking and twiddled his hair, furiously. 'Good God! I'm calmly sitting here, telling you that it's quite likely that one of my colleagues battered Miss Bland to death between finishing his early morning coffee and taking his first lesson. I don't think it's likely at all.' He gripped the plastic edge of the table with both hands and closed his eyes.

It was a melodramatic gesture but Browne didn't think it was theatrical in intent. He sat waiting for Maynard to collect himself. They were both startled by the sound of a great deal of crockery crashing to the floor. There was an instant of complete silence followed by screams of hysterical laughter.

Maynard opened his eyes. 'They're as excited as the children. It sounds as though it's a good job we shan't be needing any plates today. We'd better stop them whilst there are still a few left and before they waste any more food.' He pushed back his chair and half rose but Browne motioned him down again.

'Bellamy's seen to that. He'll be back in a minute. They're just clearing away. In the meantime, tell me which people found Miss Bland . . . "insufferable" I think you said.'

Maynard blanched and returned his gaze to the empty trolleys. 'I can't think of anyone who actually hated her but almost everybody found her irritating, lacking in the charm that oils the wheels. She made my job difficult. Sometimes it was impossible to soothe the people she'd upset. Some of them looked on me as the contrasting nice guy who'd let them do as they liked. They were unreasonably angry if I refused them as well.'

'And whom did she upset?'

'Well, yesterday, it was Julian.'

Browne looked up. 'Mr Frayn? From the English department? With the leaky biro in his pocket?'

'That's right.'

'And what was upsetting Mr Frayn?'

'It was at last night's staff meeting. There's a sixth-form girl, Valerie Kelsey, who's doing Cambridge scholarship exams this term. She was a bit of a tearaway as a youngster and consequently has a police record. Her early circumstances do a lot to excuse it and no one thinks about it any more. She's happily adopted now, hard-working, co-operative and quite brilliant. Julian thinks the school shouldn't mention her early troubles in her reference. Miss Bland disagreed. As a matter of fact, I think she was quite right. Julian's first wife died in a car crash during her first pregnancy and then, before he married Kate, he had an attack of something, mumps I think it was, with complications, and after that he couldn't have an infant of his own. I can understand why he gets a bit possessive with some of ours sometimes. Of course, Miss Bland had to declare all the facts of the case, but so many times she's put the smooth running of the machine before the best interests of the individual that people were supporting Julian in order to oppose her.' His engaging grin reappeared as he added, 'They usually do – support Julian, I mean. He's got a way with him.'

'What else was discussed at last night's staff meeting?'

'Meg Rivers complained that the entrance hall looked tatty.' Browne remembered the expiring plants and the exposed fire hose. 'And Kevin White, the PE man, said that different people on duty were applying different standards and that it should be made clear what we expected of the children. There was some talk about changing the date of school exams. Oh, and Penny Stafford was annoyed because it was impossible to get into school in the summer holidays to use library books and so on. She wanted Miss Bland to speak to the caretaker about it. That's all, I think, though it took an eternity to wade through.'

'It sounds like quite a busy programme. Will you take me through your own movements from your arrival here this morning?'

Maynard had been expecting this line of questioning and took it in his stride quite easily. 'I got here rather at the last minute, about a quarter to nine. I arrived in running gear and in rather a lather with only a few minutes to change. I grabbed a cup of tea from the staff room and took it to Kevin White's room.'

'The PE man?'

'Yes, he lets me use his shower and changing facilities. I was back in my office just after ten to. Mr Blythe and Mrs Viner came for the usual morning confab. I've told you this already. I sent them off for coffee because there was nothing to discuss and I was still getting my breath back.'

'Do you always run to school?'

Maynard smiled broadly and visibly expanded. 'That's right. It keeps Kevin in his place for one thing.'

Before this cryptic reply could be followed up, Hunter appeared in the doorway. He seemed, from his smug expression, to be tolerably satisfied with life. Browne turned to his interviewee. 'If you'll just wait here for a few minutes, Mr Maynard, whilst Sergeant Hunter and I bring each other up to date, you can then start organising your general exodus.'

Hunter preceded his chief into Mrs Weston's office but left her chair for him to occupy. Watching Browne settle himself, Hunter allowed the pleased smirk to occupy more of his face.

'You look as if you've made progress,' Browne observed. 'What's happening?'

'Out of approximately eight hundred and fifty pupils and staff in this building at the time of the killing, only eight can't prove "no opportunity".'

'Don't you think eight suspects for forensic examination is quite a lot?'

'Quite a lot better than eight hundred,' Hunter replied pertly, 'and they're all staff.'

'What? No wandering kids?'

'Only two. This seems a pretty well-ordered school. I've had a quick look round. There's no carving of initials and obscenities on the doors of the boys' loos. Very good test, that, of whether a school's discipline's up to scratch.'

'Didn't any of them have to give books in and so on?'

'They do that on the way to assembly. They have to file past the staff room to get to the hall. They stick books in the pigeon-holes outside and get back into line pronto or there's trouble.'

'You have been beavering about, haven't you? What about the two lone wanderers?'

'At least they stuck together and they hadn't got far before Maynard copped them, made them dance and sent them beetling along to rejoin their fellows. One of them's a perennial nuisance. Offspring of the head of biology, who, incidentally, is one of the aforementioned eight.'

'And the others?'

Scorning to use his notes, Hunter enumerated on his fingers. 'Miss Penny Stafford was suffering from a migraine attack. She arrived and at some point went home. Mrs Glenys Freebourne was attending to animals in the biology lab, opposite the school office. There, if you'll believe it, she was visited by her mother.'

Browne inclined his head, showing no surprise.

'Mr Kevin White was drinking tea in the staff room and then inspecting a football pitch. Mrs Meg Rivers was setting

41

up a cookery demonstration in the domestic science room, just the other side of the fire doors. Mrs Carol Weston was busy in the duplicating room on the far side of the head's study. Mr Geoffrey Maynard was dropping his running kit on his office desk to add the finishing touch to his almost perfect chaos.

'Apart from Maynard, the fond mother and Miss Stafford, they're sitting in the hall, several feet apart from each other, simmering gently and being fondly surveyed by Constable Bellamy. They aren't going to take kindly to being carted off in police cars.'

'They can take to it just as they like. Wait a minute.' Browne affected a necessity to count on his fingers. 'Six staff and one mother makes seven.'

'Yes. Mr Frayn registered his form, visited Mrs Weston and has now, unaccountably, disappeared.'

Chapter 3

Browne settled himself more comfortably in the cushioned swivel chair as he digested this information. 'So now we have two absconders, Frayn and the indisposed Miss Stafford. Do we know what happened to Mrs Freebourne's itinerant mother?'

Hunter seated himself astride the upright chair, his arms folded across its backrest and expounded. 'They assume that, having berated her daughter in her usual fashion, she departed for home. Name of Corby. She lives just round the corner from here.'

'What about non-teaching staff, caretaker, cooks and so on?'

Hunter had done his homework. 'Caretaker and head cook are man and wife. Bellamy's been grilling him whilst Maynard and I talked to the pupils. Apparently, he sat in his little cubby-hole of an office from a quarter to nine until after ten past, doing paperwork and using the phone. Certainly he answered promptly when Mrs Weston rang him, just before nine, ditto when his wife rang from the kitchen at about five past and again, just afterwards, when Mrs Freebourne asked him to bring a bucket of sand over to the corridor just beyond the fire doors here, where someone had been sick.'

'Where's his office?'

'At the other end of the bottom main corridor near the staff room. It would take him a couple of minutes to get here, and to get back he'd have to come the same way, in full view of a corridor full of staff and pupils leaving assembly, or go the long way round outside, where he'd still be seen by anyone going to either of the art rooms.'

Checking these hypothetical movements on the plan of the school hanging on the wall on his right, Browne nodded. 'All right, it's not really on. I'll allow you to eliminate him for the moment. Who's talked to the kitchen staff?'

'Bellamy again.We didn't get much joy there. He'll give you the details himself but they were all drinking tea – having a sort of breakfast-time break – for most of the relevant time. Two of them were in the kitchen making it but they can vouch for each other. When they'd finished they were all allocated tasks for today's particular meal and everyone who was given an instruction answered promptly.'

Tired of riding his chair like a horse, Hunter stood up, swung a long athletic leg over the backrest and sat on the seat with his ankles neatly crossed. 'I know Mitchell's everyone's blue-eyed boy, but Bellamy's shaping up pretty well too.'

Browne agreed, fishing in his pocket for the notebook in which he had recorded the details of school procedure he had got from Maynard. He summarised the interview. 'I only spoke to him for a few minutes. I'm surprised how disorientated he seems this morning. He didn't suggest any serious motive but he says she irritated everyone here.'

Hunter dispensed with his chair altogether and wandered over to the window. 'She may have irritated other people, parents, neighbours, a man friend,' he suggested.

'She may very well but it would have been easier for them to attack her elsewhere. Maynard pointed out how conspicuous someone is who's not supposed to be in school. I don't think an outsider would have made that difficulty for himself, though we certainly can't rule one out.'

Hunter was looking through the window. 'The four cars are here, sir. Bellamy knows he's to sit them all separately, one in front and one behind. I'll just nip out and give the fourth driver the same instructions, plus the addresses of Mrs Corby and Miss Stafford.' Glad to be on the move, physically, Hunter went outside.

Browne seemed to occupy himself with catching up on

missed sleep until his colleague reappeared, chuckling. 'They all seemed to find the proceedings a bit *infra dig* but they're submitting out of duty as good citizens. Maynard was surprised to be included and doubtful whether Blythe or Mrs Viner could organise the children's dispersal. Now he's sunk in deep gloom.'

Browne roused himself sharply. 'I hope Bellamy made it quite clear that they weren't under arrest and had the right to refuse.'

Hunter looked affronted. 'Give him credit, sir. He told them they were unfortunate in not being able to produce an alibi when they had only been following their daily duties. I pointed out that allowing us to take their clothes for examination gave them an opportunity to help to eliminate themselves. I've reminded Bellamy to enter them in the non-casual-visitors' book and to inform Thaxton that they're there. Thaxton is still acting custody officer, isn't he? Burns doesn't come back till next Monday?'

Browne nodded. 'Fair enough. And can Blythe and Mrs Viner cope in Maynard's absence?'

'They seem to think so. Anyway, they'll have to. Mrs Viner's busy talking to the governors and is going to tackle the kitchen staff. Blythe's requesting the co-operation of the transport people. The press has arrived, by the way, and is making a nuisance of itself at the gate.'

As they considered the information they had gleaned so far, each man concentrated in his own way. Browne sat, motionless, his broad forehead furrowed, his lean, square jaw tightened. Hunter prowled restlessly in the narrow space between the teak-veneered cupboards that stood against one long wall and the grey metal filing cabinets ranged along the other. There was silence as each of them tried to see in which direction their next enquiries should lead.

Presently, Browne raised his head. 'Let's sum up so far. Ledgard has given us a rough picture of what went on next door. Someone was in the room with her who gave her no reason to be on her guard. She sat at her desk with her back to her visitor. Perhaps she was checking something on one of the lists on the notice-board above the desk, or in one of the letters on the desk itself.'

'She may have turned her back to dismiss the visitor, or as a calculated snub,' Hunter suggested.

'Could be. The cat seems to have been the weapon. Its shape is consistent with the wounds inflicted and Ledgard has explained the absence of blood on it. I wonder if that was deliberate.'

'If what was?'

'The wounds being inflicted on different sites. If I was battering someone's head in and wanting to kill them as quickly as possible before I was interrupted, I think I'd keep hitting the same place.'

Hunter paused in his prowling to consider. 'Perhaps the murderer beat in the same direction and she struggled and turned her head.'

'Could be,' Browne said again, 'but Ledgard doesn't think so. Maybe our man had counted on the crushed blood vessels not bleeding too much so that he'd emerge unmarked himself.'

'Are we to confine our enquiries to males with a detailed knowledge of physiology?'

'I think not.' Browne looked hard at his Sergeant who gazed innocently back. 'The only suggestion Ledgard has made about the identity of the attacker is that he, or she, is almost certainly right-handed.'

Hunter shut his eyes to re-create in his mind the earlier scenes in the office. Browne waited, watching a shaft of sun pick out the aquiline features of his colleague's narrow face. The tightened mouth made his thin lips thinner and the sunlight washed out what colour there usually was in the pale face and fine, fair-brown hair. Presently, the eyes opened, rich brown and alert and the face became animated and intelligent again.

'Mrs Weston is,' Hunter announced, 'and Maynard. Mrs Viner's left-handed and I don't think Mr Blythe gave us any evidence to judge by.'

Browne accepted and was thankful for Hunter's almost

total recall. He himself lacked any such unusual or peculiarly useful attributes and had attained his present rank by the exercise of only a formidable common sense. He closed his notebook. 'I think, for the moment, we'll accept Blythe's and Mrs Viner's alibis for each other. That leaves us eight prize beauties to question when the forensic people have finished with them. And since we can't get at them at the moment, we'll look around here a bit. We can't go next door until the SOCO boys give us the all-clear. You take this place, Jerry. Give it a thorough going over and save the choice bits to share with me. I want to have a prowl around the staff room.'

He watched as Hunter, starting on his allotted task, pulled open the top drawer of a filing cabinet. 'Everyone except the killer went off to first lesson leaving possessions about and jobs half finished, expecting to be back at morning break, and with no idea that we'd be poking about. I'll see what I can find out about them all before they're allowed back in to remove and change things. When we've both finished, we'll have a go at the head's study together. Keep your eyes open in case Mr Frayn deigns to reappear. If he does, hole him up somewhere on his own.'

Approaching the fire doors leading to the main corridor, Browne found them opened for him by Bellamy, who was passing the time in conversation with Dean. 'If you've time to talk, young Nigel, you can do a spot of guard duty yourself. Go and relieve Mitchell at the outside door and send him to me in the staff room.'

'Yes, sir. Will he know where it is?'

'He ought to. He's stood outside it often enough, waiting for retribution for his various sins.'

Grinning to himself at the barely concealed malevolence displayed by the unrelieved and indignant Dean, Browne took himself off. In approximately the place he expected, he found a scarlet-painted door labelled 'Staff Room'. Beneath the label, a large cardboard notice, fixed with drawing pins, announced, inhospitably, that pupils were to knock only in the case of dire emergency. The room behind it was pleasantly sunlit. The walls, where they were not plastered with notices, were a cheerful yellow and the curtains patterned in brown and gold. An attempt had been made to make the large space seem more friendly by arranging armless easy chairs to form two large squares. Several low tables stood inside the squares, whilst a row of higher ones, evidently used for marking and other paperwork, ran across the back of the room in front of the windows.

The leaves of the beech tree growing just outside would have aptly complemented the colour scheme if window-sills, piled high with books and papers, had not almost totally obscured the view. In fact, every surface in the room had been commandeered to hold files, exercise books, maps, boxes of chalk and all the rest of a teaching staff's impedimenta.

When Mitchell tapped on the door and came in, he found Browne in rapt contemplation of a table on which stood an ancient Banda machine, a collection of plastic carrier bags full of assorted toys, shoes and grubby garments, and, in a space at the front, roughly cleared for them, a stack of stained fibre boxes, containing, Browne estimated, about ten dozen eggs.

Mitchell answered the unspoken question. 'The carrier bags are lost property, sir. Mr Blythe brings them out on to a trestle table in the foyer on Friday lunch-times and you're invited to make a contribution to the school fund when you collect what you've lost.'

'And if you decline?'

'I don't know, sir. The only time I had to claim something, Mr Blythe was away and Mr White was substituting for him. When I was pushing my trainers back in my bag, he said, "You were offering a reward for them, weren't you, Mitchell?" and I paid up.' He added, reminiscently, and with feeling, 'People usually do what Mr White wants.'

Brown nodded. 'And the eggs?'

'That's Jim Barstow, the caretaker, sir. He's got a hen coop in his back garden. He sells the eggs in school and feeds the birds on the waste food his wife brings from the kitchen. She's the cook here. And we always said Mrs Freebourne got a few free eggs for turning a blind eye when old Barstow helped himself from the stuff for the school animals.'

'What animals?'

'Well, the biology department has had various ones over the years, although I think there's only locusts and bees at the moment. The rural science class has a couple of goats, though. They're in the field next to the playground. There's a shed for when the weather's bad.'

'And what day is the goats' milk on sale?'

Mitchell wondered whether to laugh but decided not to. 'It isn't, sir, as far as I know.'

Turning his back on the table, Browne surveyed a collection of lockers which backed on to a wall. He pulled open one on the top row and studied its contents. Everything was painfully neat. The top shelf contained copies of *A Winter's Tale*, *Men and Women*, the complete works of Chaucer in one volume and *Religio Medici* by Sir Thomas Browne. The Inspector picked out the volume by his namesake and riffled through the India paper pages. There were various marginal notes and observations, written in a hand as neat and legible as the printed text. He replaced the book, glanced at the tidy pile of file paper and the bottle of red fountain-pen ink on the lower shelf, then closed the door.

Mitchell had been looking over his shoulder feeling rather like a naughty schoolboy trespassing on his teachers' territory for a dare. 'I knew that would be Frayn's,' he observed, having checked the name stamped into the aluminium strip on the door. 'He's the only one who uses an old-fashioned pen and no one else is so tidy. Let's have a look in old Stafford's. Everything'll probably fall out of hers.'

'This is a murder investigation,' Browne reminded him, 'not a prank.' Nevertheless, he opened Miss Stafford's locker and, as Mitchell had foretold, a bottle of cough linctus, a packet of tissues, a creased woollen jacket and a bottle of aspirins cascaded to the floor. 'Our resident valetudinarian,' Browne remarked.

Mitchell blinked and remained silent as he helped to stow away Miss Stafford's possessions more securely. Browne pulled open all the remaining lockers, leaving their contents on view. The one at the far end, belonging to Kevin White, contained an open packet of contraceptives. Browne regarded it quizzically. 'I see this isn't a staff that rushes home straight after last lesson.'

Mindful of the snub Browne had just administered, Mitchell kept his face straight and suggested, 'Its most likely been confiscated, sir, or used to illustrate a talk on AIDS.' Then he realised that this time he was allowed to laugh and did so. He pushed a precariously balanced jar of instant coffee further on to the shelf in the same locker and, at a nod from his chief, closed the doors of all of them. He joined Browne, who was now surveying the untidy corner of the room to the right of the door.

Their observation of it was interrupted by the entry of a man in shirt-sleeves, an academic gown over his arm. Browne contemplated the fresh-complexioned, intelligent face, the thinning grey-brown curls and the questioning hazel eyes. Their owner addressed the junior officer.

'Hello, Benny. I gather there's been an incident.'

Instead of replying, Mitchell turned to his Inspector. 'It's Mr Frayn, sir.'

Frayn transferred his attention to Browne. 'What's happened? Has there been an accident?'

He made to sit down on the nearest chair, but a swift gesture from Browne stopped him.

'I'd like you to remain standing where you are for a few moments, Mr Frayn. To answer your question, it was hardly an accident. Someone has killed Miss Bland. Several of your colleagues have left for the police station to assist us there. I'm afraid I have to invite you to join them.'

Frayne gave a delighted smile. 'Certainly. I always enjoy new experiences. But I won't be much help to you. I wasn't even there.'

Browne made no comment on this seemingly callous reaction. He could see that the man was shaken. 'Precisely. Where were you?' Leaving him to consider his answer, Browne turned to Mitchell. 'Is there a newspaper somewhere in this chaos?'

Mitchell looked around him and Frayn bridled. 'Unfair, Chief Inspector.' He glanced at Browne's face and corrected himself. 'Inspector?' Browne nodded and Frayn smiled. 'Never mind, I erred on the right side.' He indicated the untidy corner. Cardboard boxes were stacked there, purporting to contain Scotch whisky and table margarine and plastered with exhortations to the grocer to use in rotation and keep this way up. 'It may look like a supermarket warehouse,' Frayn admitted, 'but, actually, the boxes are full of old exam scripts, which none of us want or will ever refer to again. They're waiting for the statutory period to elapse before they can be destroyed and replaced by similar redundant litter. And these surfaces' – his gesture indicated the heaped-up tables, chairs and window-sills – 'may look cluttered, but, considering what has to be kept in here, we do well to remember where we've put everything and keep the system going.'

Mitchell produced a copy of *The Times* and spread it over the seat and backrest of the nearest chair. Browne indicated that the master might be seated on it and repeated his question.

Frayn settled himself. 'I went home, Inspector. The first two periods on Wednesday are free for me. I left assembly, which was even more pointless and disorganised than usual, and returned to the bosom of my wife. I couldn't have behaved more suspiciously, could I? Having committed the crime, you are no doubt thinking, I spent long enough in the somewhat perfunctory morning service to feel shriven, then rushed to my house, which is, conveniently, just across the road, to get rid of my gun, or my piece of rope, or my bloodstained butcher's knife. Than I drank black coffee till my hands had stopped shaking and my teeth chattering and sauntered back to ask you why a policeman at the gate was too busy turning away the press to see me slip, in my customary fashion, through the gap in the hedge.'

Frayn's voice faltered, then stopped. He shifted on the chair and the newspaper crackled under him. Both he and Browne were aware of Mitchell's mixture of amusement and astonishment at his behaviour. When he spoke again, it was with a more subdued demeanour and tone. 'I'm sorry, Inspector. I'm just beginning to take it in. I'm not talking this nonsense because I don't care.'

'It's a reaction I've seen before, Mr Frayn. I won't read too much into it. Was the bosom of your wife at home for you to return to?'

'Yes. It was Kate who noticed the police presence and said I'd better get back. But what really happened to Miss Bland? Couldn't it have been an accident? And why am I sitting on yesterday's *Times*?'

Browne smiled. 'You needn't any longer.' He turned to Mitchell. 'We'd better not send for another squad car. That would be pushing our luck. You can take Mr Frayn down to the station.' He answered Mitchell's anguished expression with a glare. 'Get back here as quickly as you can.' The reluctant Constable escorted his suspect to the car and Browne returned to his scrutiny of the staff room.

Union posters about teachers' pay and conditions adorned the remaining wall and urged members to adopt various attitudes. This was obviously a politically minded staff and he speculated that union activity would be weaker in a happier school. The large notice-board afforded him a bewildering assortment of cryptic initials. He was defeated after some thought by only one and determined to consult Maynard at some future date on the mysteries of TVEI.

When Mitchell returned, some twenty-five minutes later, Browne had finished his prowling. It seemed to him that the young Constable had something on his mind. 'Anything strike you so far, Mitchell?'

'Well, sir, just that Mr Frayn seemed to rush in and accuse himself to stop us doing it first. And then . . . '

'Go on.'

52

'Well, sir, when he was giving us a list of ways he could have committed the crime, it was interesting that he didn't mention the most obvious one that actually was used.'

Browne bit his lip. 'The psychological approach, eh? That's hardly enough to base a conviction on but it's an interesting observation. How did you and Mr Frayn entertain each other on the journey down?'

'It was a bit awkward, sir. Mostly we talked about people who were in my school year who still keep in touch.'

Trying the telephone on the table in front of him, Browne found that it got him straight through to the office. Mitchell listened in to his half of the conversation. 'I've finished here. How are you getting on?' Hunter replied at length and Browne made brief notes. 'Carry on there, then. Yes, that was Frayn. I'm going to pop over the road and see what his wife has to tell us. I'll come across to you after that. I'll take Mitchell with me.'

Thick lips parted in a delighted grin. 'Great stuff, sir. Mrs Frayn is something else again and I've been dying to see old Frayn's set-up.'

Browne's black eyebrows met in a scowl that made him look like one of the smaller varieties of the monkey family. 'You're still behaving like a schoolboy, Mitchell. Grow up if you want me to take you seriously – and your shorthand had better be up to scratch.' He swept through the door and was halfway across the foyer before Mitchell had caught up with him.

As they crossed the road, Mitchell pointed to Frayn's house, which stood back from and interrupted a row of council houses in all states of repair from spruce and shining to sordid. Frayn's house was only a little shabby, its garden well planned and only a little unkempt. The path led to a grey-green panelled door that toned pleasantly with the walls of local millstone grit which in turn made an attractive contrast with the neighbours' red brick.

Before they had time to knock, the door was opened by a slightly built girl with a freckled face on which the anxious expression it wore looked out of place. The wide mouth seemed a more suitable vehicle for a gamine grin. She wore crumpled but clean drill jeans and the thick fair hair, though it had been pushed untidily off her face, was well brushed.

She stepped back to allow them to enter the hall, moving with the careless grace of those lucky teenagers who remain thin but escape gawkiness. She took them into a sitting-room and indicated a comfortable chair from which she removed part of a typed manuscript to enable Browne to sit in it. Mitchell took an upright chair by the door.

The room, with its film of dust and its scattering of magazines and papers, displayed a casual disregard for the niceties of housekeeping, but certainly not fecklessness. As she stood in the full sunlight Browne could now see that she was probably in her thirties but still considerably younger than her husband. Except for her brief 'Come in' none of them had spoken. She sat on the chair opposite Browne.

'I've been watching out of the window since Julian went back,' she told him. 'What's happened over there?'

Browne was surprised by the deep voice. 'I take it you're Mrs Frayn.' She nodded. 'I'm Detective Inspector Browne. I'm afraid I must ask the questions at this stage.'

'At this stage of what?'

As though she had not interrupted, he continued. 'What time was it when your husband returned from school this morning?'

She thought for a moment. 'Just before a quarter past nine. I'm not sure to the minute. I was in the attic.'

'Did you hear him come in?'

'I heard some movement downstairs and as I was coming to investigate, he called to me from the lower landing.'

'Were you surprised to see him?'

'I wasn't expecting him but I wasn't astonished. I knew he had no lessons before break this morning.'

'What did he tell you he'd come for?'

She blushed, the freckles drowning in a wave of crimson. Staring at her knees, she told him, 'To make up the quarrel we had at breakfast-time.'

'Was it serious?'

She considered. 'It seemed so at the time but it wasn't marriage-shattering. He hadn't come to see if I was packing a case. Look, I'll explain exactly what happened. He's always irritable first thing in the morning. That's when my rather slipshod housekeeping annoys him. When I got up, I rushed up to the study to scribble up an idea and so breakfast was late. I try to write, you see. I suppose if I'd written a couple of great novels he'd think my shortcomings were justified, but for my first serious book it's even more important to catch the ideas as they come. Anyway, this morning he threw my romance at me.'

Browne's eyebrows shot up and she smiled. 'Not literally. He can win all his fights with words and quick thinking. He never has to resort to anything physical.'

'So what did you mean?'

She blushed again. 'When I gave up teaching to write full time we were hard up, so I wrote a silly romance to make some money before I tried any serious work. As an academic exercise, although it certainly wasn't academic. I quite enjoyed writing at a level that tells the reader what to feel, what to think and what to see. When I was typing it out I blushed for it, and yet, at the same time, I wasn't ashamed. I felt a bit like a professional dressmaker, who's made a garment in execrable taste but made it well out of good-quality material. Anyway Julian said he wasn't having his domestic life disrupted when all I produced was that kind of thing. He knows I only did it to keep us solvent, but I think he thought he'd really hurt me, suggesting that that was all I was capable of.'

'Did it take him an hour to apologise?'

Her face was crimson again. 'He asked me if the inspiration was flowing and I told him it was hard going this morning. Then he said if I came down he'd apologise. When I got to the first landing, he was standing there with nothing on. He said, "When I say I'm sorry, I do it properly. You ought to know that by now." Then' – she bit her lip – 'he took me into the bedroom and made love to me.'

'Had he bathed or showered?'

She forgot her embarrassment in irritation. 'Does it matter to anyone else?' Browne waited for his answer and after a few seconds she continued. 'He may have. He was coming out of the bathroom as I came down.' Suddenly her irritation increased. 'Look, Julian started to get dressed again just after ten. Whilst he finished, I went down in my dressing-gown and made some coffee. As we drank it we noticed your squad cars across the road, Now it's your turn. Tell me what you're investigating and what it's got to do with what Julian and I were doing over here.'

He told her bluntly. Her eyes widened and betrayed her horror, but she sat still, absorbing the news, and regained her composure before she spoke again. 'Poor Sarah. She didn't deserve that.' This was the first expression of sorrow Browne had heard; the first use, too, of Miss Bland's Christian name. Suddenly, Kate Frayn looked alarmed. 'Do you think Julian had anything to do with it? Where is he now?' Her voice rose and she paused again to control it.

Browne slipped another question into the silence. 'Was your husband's behaviour this morning typical of him?'

She had a grip on herself again and answered him evenly. 'Love-making during the day isn't. An extravagant gesture to end a quarrel is.'

Suddenly realising with what difficulty his witness was maintaining her control, he was sorry for her. 'We needn't trouble you much longer. Just a couple more questions. Did your husband go back to school in the same clothes he came home in?'

She shrugged. 'All his school clothes are much alike. I expect he did. He wore just his shirt and tie because his jacket pocket got stained with biro ink. He said Carol Weston was getting it out for him. He had his gown with him but he wasn't wearing it. It's quite warm for September, once the early morning chill has worn off.' She sat, staring, unseeing, in front of her.

Browne looked at her. He had never understood how women could be classified as beautiful or ugly on such criteria as body shape, physiognomy or colouring. To him, their features conveyed an alert mind and a unique personality and they were attractive, or else they failed to do so and were not. His wife, Hannah, was beautiful by this definition, and Kate Frayn's features did not fail. He remembered Mitchell's phrase, 'something else again', and tacitly commended his Constable's discrimination, if not his terminology.

'I'd be grateful if, before we go, you'd let us have a look round the bedroom and bathroom.'

Her voice was colourless. 'I've no choice but to let you, have I?' She nodded her permission but remained in her chair, leaving them to find their own way. When they had left the room, she grabbed a pencil and began to scribble in an exercise book. Reaching the bottom of the page, she ripped it out and folded it.

Some minutes later, as the two policemen were taking their leave, she pushed it into Browne's hand. 'That's my answer to the question you didn't ask,' she told Browne coolly.

He put a hand on her arm, turning her back towards them. 'Your husband's down at the station letting our forensic people examine him. I might tell you that out of eight people given the same treatment, he was the only one who had the sense not to protest.'

She shook off his hand and turned away. When they left, she closed the door quickly behind them.

'Looks bad for him, doesn't it, sir?' Mitchell carefully closed the gate and hurried after the Inspector.

Browne's tone was phlegmatic. 'Could do. Let's get back and see what the lady wanted to be asked.'

Chapter 4

During his conversation with Mrs Frayn, a fraction of Browne's mind had been aware of service buses passing the window, first empty and then full of children. The atmosphere in the school when they returned was much altered. The car park now held less than a dozen vehicles and the building had lost its busy hum. The door swung to behind them and its slam echoed along the empty tiled and painted corridors.

Browne paused to read the sheet of paper in his hand and Mitchell, longing but not daring to look over his shoulder, held the fire door open for him instead. Browne refolded the paper, left Mitchell to make his peace with Dean and went into the office. He found the Sergeant seated behind the desk, also perusing a sheet of paper, and regarded him affectionately. Hunter's face was long and thin, the eyes, neatly browed, set close together and the mouth small. He recalled Kate Frayn's wide grin which, from time to time during his interview with her, had lit up her whole face. Hunter was physically incapable of grinning but Browne knew from experience that this particular arrangement of his features meant that he was pleased.

He sat, in a dignified fashion, on the chair that Hunter had ridden. 'Had an interesting morning, Jeremy?'

'Quite interesting, sir. There's a lot of standard equipment here that we needn't bother with. Those cupboards are full of spare stationery and duplicating stencils. The grey cabinet contains pupils' records in alphabetical order of each year. The little cupboard on the wall has their coffee-making equipment. They do themselves well, freshly ground coffee and long-life cream. The photocopier in the corner is in good order. The big Gestetner for large numbers of reprints is in a little office-cum-cupboard at the other side of the head's room. It's obviously been used this morning. In fact, I should think the fumes are still strong enough to be dangerous. There were trays of papers on top of that cabinet. One has shorthand copies or rough handwritten drafts of letters waiting to be typed. The other three are labelled "Caught", "Bowled", and "LBW". Someone's obviously a cricketer.'

'And what have we in these originally labelled trays?'

'An interesting assortment. "LBW" has two applications from staff to go on courses in school time. "Caught" has two requests from local firms for references for pupils they are considering for employment and a letter from the parent of a third-year boy, complaining that he has been assaulted by our friend Miss Stafford.'

'The invalid lady has attacked a boy?'

'So it would appear.'

'And what's in "Bowled"?'

'A reply to the assaulted boy's parents, saying the matter will be thoroughly investigated and inviting them to come into school. Then there's a Cambridge University reference for a girl who, in its writer's opinion, is a genius, a leader of men – and women, presumably – and a paragon of virtue. However, there is a handwritten note, initialled, I think, by Miss Bland, to the effect that this document makes no mention of her police record. The girl's, I mean.'

'The plot thickens. Is that all?'

'Nearly.' Hunter's moment of glory was almost over and his mouth was buttoned again. 'There are eight identical copies of a letter of complaint about lack of effort and uncooperative behaviour with a space left for the relevant pupil's name. They're filled in and one is destined for the Freebournes, to the detriment of the illustrious Neville.'

'Ah, yes. One of the duo who preferred a quick drag

to their morning devotions. We'd better follow that lot up. What's the pile of stuff on the corner of the desk?'

'There's the admissions book. Each pupil in it has a roll number. It's a sort of guide to all that stuff in the cabinets. The fat book contains the accounts of all the different monies the secretary deals with. They seem to be in apple-pie order. Then, finally, there's the signing-out book, which, incidentally, Frayn omitted to adorn with his name.'

'Possibly he jibbed at filling in "Reason for being out of school",' Browne suggested.

'What was his reason?'

Browne leaned back in his chair and gave Hunter a summary of his interview with Mrs Frayn. Hunter fiddled with his pen as he listened, then held out his hand for the sheet of paper Browne handed to him. He read it in silence, then raised questioning eyes to Browne.

'Is it some kind of intellectual joke?' Looking back at the paper, he reread it, forming the words aloud. 'Asked about her husband's relationship with Miss Bland, Kate was obliged to examine it. She knew him to be one of the few members of staff who had found something in her that he could genuinely like. He was so sure of himself – and Sarah wasn't a person who could be popular with people who were looking for a sense of security from their relationships. She wasn't either soothing or sympathetic but nor was she insensitive. Julian was a sort of substitute father to her, though a woman in her early forties should not have required him in this role. How was she to convey any of this to the Inspector? He would hear only of the tooth and nail fights between Julian and Sarah over matters of principle in school. He'd want to know what kind of matters. Well, there was what she called the "moral tone" of the school magazine and whether *A Winter's Tale* was suitable material for a school production. Really, Sarah was a bit of a prude.'

Hunter dropped the scrap of paper back on the desk. 'Is she making a novel out of the affair before it's more than begun?'

The cleft in Browne's chin became more pronounced. 'I think she has the writer's habit of observing rather than involving herself in a direct confrontation. She wanted to defend her husband and as I didn't give her a suitable opening, she took the initiative and used the method that suited her best.'

Hunter handed back the sheet and Browne put it away in his notebook.

'Did you find anything in the bedroom or bathroom, sir?'

'Just an interesting clash of personalities. There was fluff under the bed and Mrs Frayn's bedside table was littered with books and papers. Mr Frayn's had one book and no dust. The bathroom was clean but untidy, except that all the damp towels were neatly hung to dry. I think he'd tidied hers when he hung his own. I had a good sort through the dirty linen basket, of course. Nothing of interest there and the sink he'd used was spotless.'

Hunter pushed back his chair and was about to resume his habitual prowl when the telephone rang. He answered it and handed over the receiver to Browne who listened, expressed his thanks and rang off. 'The London people have contacted Miss Bland's family,' he told Hunter. 'Apparently her father had a heart attack last night and isn't to be told anything for the moment. The mother wants to stay with him, at least until the PM and the inquest are over and something can be done about the funeral. We've a number to contact her if we need her. They've interviewed her, but understandably, they don't feel they can push her too far at the moment. They're sending their report. I'll look at it as soon as it comes and see her for myself as soon as I've done what's most pressing at this end.'

He went to the door and put his head into the corridor. Mitchell caught his eye and came through the fire doors, his expression eager. Browne's remarks changed it. 'I've given you time to re-establish diplomatic relations with Dean. Go and give Bellamy a break and send him in here, will you?' Mitchell knew better than to argue and disappeared towards the far end of the corridor.

As they waited for Bellamy to appear, the two senior officers heard sounds from the next room of voices and equipment being shifted about, suggesting that the Scenes of Crime Officers were still busy. Browne popped his head round the door. 'Keeping you busy, is it? How long before we can poke around in here?'

Swann was kneeling in front of the desk, taking photographs of stains on the carpet where blood had dripped from the desk. Satisfied that he had enough satisfactory shots of it, he removed the white arrow with which Donaldson had indicated it and paused to answer before creeping round the side of the desk to the next one. 'I reckon it'll be another hour or so before we can clear out of your way. The mortuary van's on its way. We're just about to bag up the head and so on.'

Browne smiled at his agonised expression as he wriggled himself into a convenient position to take the next photograph. 'Happy hunting, then. We'll amuse ourselves elsewhere for a bit longer.'

He closed the door connecting the two rooms as Bellamy tapped on the one in the corridor. The cool wind now blowing across the playground had reddened the Constable's cheeks and nose and stiffened his jaw but had not abated his enthusiasm. Browne congratulated him on his efficient interrogation of the caretaker and his minions. 'Have you anything to add to your official report, Bellamy? Any gut feelings or general impressions – off the record?'

Bellamy assumed an expression of profound thought, so that his comment, when it came, was an anticlimax. 'The caretaker's wife's a bit of a character, sir. Doesn't miss much and speaks a language all her own. Needs an interpreter, really.'

'Right then, wheel her in. We could do with a bit of light relief.' Seeing the Constable's face fall, he added, 'No reflection on your efforts with her about the kitchen staff, but, if you think she knows all about the set-up here, I'll take your advice and let her gossip to us.'

His ruffled feathers smooth again, Bellamy departed to

recall his witness. He was soon back and she made an entrance behind him.

She was a woman of about forty who, Browne suspected, had once been an exceedingly pretty teenager and didn't seem able to adjust to being any older. She wore a loose wrap-round cotton overall in bright blue, held together by a plastic belt at least four inches wide and tightly buckled, as though it had caught the once-girlish figure in an act of indiscretion and punished it. Her face was covered with a thick layer of pancake make-up, in a brave attempt to obliterate her creator's lack of continuing care and leave a blank canvas on which to re-draw the face she used to have. Her natural complexion, which showed at the edges, was still fair enough for her to have got away with restoring her hair to the blonde it had once been but not to the blonde she had chosen for it. The front was cut short in a fringe over her forehead and its curl had been getting the worst of a battle with the kitchen steam. The rest of her hair was long, drawn tightly to the top of her head and secured in a pony-tail which continued to go upwards for a couple of inches before cascading down her back. It reminded Browne of a garden fountain.

She beamed at him with a silver-pink mouth and Browne warmed to her immediately, recognising in the direct confrontation of her spiky-lashed eyes an uncompromising witness. Bellamy drew up a chair for her and the three policemen watched her sit down. Unabashed, she crossed her legs, revealing an area of energetically patterned Crimplene between the skirts of her overall.

Since Browne still did not speak, she began the interview herself. 'I'm gettin' star treatment from the p'lice, I must say. First I 'ave the best-lookin' one, then the top brass send for me.'

Browne was enjoying watching Bellamy squirm when the telephone rang. His witness paused to run her eyes speculatively over Hunter as he answered it. Hunter blushed and turned to face the window as he listened. 'It's the station, sir. They'll have finished with the crowd down there by about one o'clock. They want to know where you want to talk to them.'

'Is there plenty of cell accommodation available?' Hunter enquired, then nodded.

'Right, then, they can cool their heels for a bit longer and I'll have them brought up here for half past.'

Hunter passed on the instructions and Browne turned back to Mrs Barstow.

'Before we begin the interview, I wonder if I can ask you a favour. I want to bring some of the staff back to school this afternoon and they won't have been fed. Do you think you could produce some sort of cold meal for nine or ten people in the staff room at one thirty?'

Mrs Barstow had come to be obliging and availed herself of this opportunity. 'It'll be a pleasure, sir. We've stuck a lot of the stuff for today's meal back in the freezers but there's plenty of oddments that want using up. Them 'aving it'll be better than wasting it.' She didn't add, 'but only just,' though her tone implied it. 'You've come to the best person, sir, if you want to know what goes on in this place. Me and them prefects keep this place going. When they're not shut up in their classrooms the staff all disappear into that staff room. What they don't see they don't 'ave to deal with.'

It struck her that, in some cases, she'd been unfair and she allowed a few exceptions. 'Mr Frayn's different. 'E's allus busy with plays and such like. 'E's got a good dodge, though. 'E sings along the corridors and the kids 'ear 'im comin' and watch out for theirselves. At least 'is voice sounds all right, though. My Jim used to sing as 'e worked round the buildin'. Unfortunately 'e were only a good singer afore tunes came out. Mrs Muck told 'im off about it.'

'Mrs Muck?'

'That Miss Bland, I mean. Allus dishin' out 'er orders. Thinks she's it wi' a capital I. Well, she used to, I mean.' Mrs Barstow made the correction out of respect for accuracy rather than the dead. 'There's other exceptions as well,' she allowed, returning to her theme of teachers' scamped responsibilities. 'That Mr White prances around like a gallopin' 'atpin wi' 'is football.' She leaned back, enjoying herself. ' 'Alf of 'em aren't much use when they are about the place. There was two littl'uns fightin' on the bottom corridor last week and that Miss Stafford was standin' at the other end, like someone who was sent for and couldn't go. Mr Maynard 'eard the row from 'is room.'

Browne gathered from the omission of the derisive 'that' before his name that Maynard commanded Mrs Barstow's respect.

' 'E soon sorted 'em out. They don't dare to misbe'ave when 'e's around. I gave Madam Stafford a look as I walked past to show 'er what I thought of 'er. She said, "I could hear the noise but I wasn't sure which direction it was coming from." ' Mrs Barstow snorted and abandoned the attempt at BBC English she had assumed to quote Miss Stafford. 'She must think I came down on t'up train! 'Er mother must 'ave drilled it into 'er that idleness's no good unless it's well carried out.'

Bellamy scribbled furiously, whilst Hunter and Browne sat perfectly still, fearing to distract her and stem the flow. After a short pause for thought, Mrs Barstow went on again.

'You might find out what that Freebourne kid was up to. I saw 'im disappearin' into the cloakroom just as I 'eard the organ startin'. Course, 'is mother won't 'ear owt against 'im. 'E's like the little white 'en that never lays away but its egg's allus found.'

Browne didn't dare meet Hunter's eye and looked down to control his amusement. Taking this as a gesture of dismissal, Mrs Barstow rose. 'Ah, well. Better shake myself and give t'chickens a feed.'

Not knowing whether this was meant literally or whether it was another of her colourful metaphors, Browne rose with her and shook her hand. 'Mrs Barstow, I've never had a witness like you,' he said, with perfect truth. 'You anticipated my every question and answered before I asked. I'd say you'd been very helpful, except that people always take that as having a sinister meaning. What are you going to give them all for lunch?' He didn't want her to forget his request.

She grinned and shrugged her thickening shoulders. 'Three runs round t'table and a kick at t'cellar door, maybe.'

A loud and tuneless singing, which Browne presumed to come from her husband, could be heard floating up the corridor. 'Oh, Lord!' The pencilled brows disappeared under the lacquered fringe. 'He's broke out in a fresh place.' She made a splendid exit, slamming the door behind her.

Hunter waited, straight-faced, whilst his chief indulged his pent-up mirth and wiped his eyes. After a few seconds, the door reopened and the brassy head reappeared. 'I just thought I'd warn you. If them things of Mrs Weston's aren't back in place before she comes in, there'll be a right old barney.'

Seeing that Browne was still submerged under his handkerchief, Hunter thanked her for the warning, but explained, 'Mrs Weston will have to realise that a murder investigation takes precedence over her convenience.'

Mrs Barstow grinned at him. 'More strength to your elbow, then. Glad you found something to say for yourself.' This time, she departed for good.

Hunter's face at being given this short shrift set off fresh peals of laughter from Browne. When he had finally recovered himself, he put away his notebook and reached for his coat. 'Come on, Jerry. Our powers of deduction will probably benefit from a change of scene. There's quite a good pub across the road. I'm afraid Virginia is familiar with it. There's an aching void in my stomach that won't be offset even by the counter-irritation of stubbing my toe whilst assaulting cellar doors.'

It was pleasant to be outside again and, in the sheltered area screened by the projecting dining and kitchen block, the sun shone warmly on their shoulders. Browne stood with his back to the building and surveyed the ridiculous tilt of the land on the north side of the town which had

66

confined its size and provided it with a moorland background of hazy purples, greens and browns. His gaze travelled down into the valley where the buildings huddled under a smoky haze. Here and there a church spire, mill chimney or pylon made a vertical line up through it, and to his right, three tower blocks thrust aggressively skywards, catching the sun and glimmering whitely. In the foreground sprawled the housing estate that surrounded the school. It consisted of ugly, square houses of orange-red brick, roofed with large, clumsy-looking tiles that seemed out of proportion to the area they covered and to the height of the dwellings. Immediately in front of him was the gravelled run-up to the jumping pit, ending in a sand-filled hollow, marked with the clear indentations made by the soles of sports shoes which had recently run across it.

Browne became aware that Hunter was forty yards in front, waiting for him and hugging himself to keep warm. He rounded the block and strode out to join him. From the shelter of the trees by the gate, two young men emerged, hopefully. One carried a notebook, the other a camera. Browne gave them a greeting but nothing more. 'You've had your money's worth out of the kids, I don't doubt. There won't be anything more till this evening at the earliest.' The men shrugged and went back to sit on the wall as the two policemen crossed the road.

A fresh breeze blew in their faces and by the time they reached the Owl, although the sun was still lifting their spirits, they were not tempted to sit at the tables set out beside the car park. They went in and settled themselves in a plush-seated bay, near to one of the brightly burning open fires. Hunter, who was unfamiliar to the barman, went to order their two halves of bitter.

The pub was not crowded and such customers as there were applied themselves to their well-filled plates and quiet conversation. Hunter brought the beer to their table and sat down opposite Browne. 'It's been a bit frustrating so far. It's useful to have all this forensic evidence but it's a nuisance to have to wait all this time to begin the interrogation. And Swann and Donaldson are taking ages.'

Browne drank, thirstily. 'I can use this. It's good stuff, too. Sit down, Jerry, and take a breather whilst you can. We haven't done so badly this morning, anyway. We've narrowed down to eight the people with a reasonable opportunity and we may have incontrovertible evidence against one of them by this afternoon.'

Hunter subsided moodily and applied himself to his glass.

Two lately arrived customers, bursting with the information that there was police activity across at the school, took their beer and their news over to the general company. Meanwhile the landlord presented himself at the policemen's table to pick up what bits of information he could, and, incidentally, to take their order. The pub offered a choice of only two dishes but the food was well prepared and good value for money. Browne decided on steak and kidney pie and Hunter on ham salad. Both men owed their lean build to a large expenditure of nervous energy. Browne enjoyed food and ate what he fancied. Hunter chose always with discrimination and even then selected, fastidiously, from what his plate contained.

They added to their order a recital of the bare facts of their case and a request that the landlord would pass on anything he heard which might be helpful to them. He nodded self-importantly and produced their lunch in short order. Finding his pie to his satisfaction, Browne was silent whilst he gave it the attention it deserved. Hunter trimmed the fat from a succulent slice of ham and carefully removed the stalk from four quarters of a tomato. When Browne, his plate cleared, laid down his knife and fork, Hunter followed suit, though almost half of his food remained. Browne indicated Hunter's empty glass. 'Want another?'

Hunter shook his head. 'It's going to be a long afternoon. I'll get us some coffee.' He wandered off to the counter.

Browne drummed his fingers on the table and looked around him. The other customers were mostly sitting with their backs to him and producing a busy hum of conversation but covert glances told him that the doings of Hunter and himself constituted the topic of it. He disregarded them and turned his attention to the wall decorations above them. Framed, beside the door, hung a poster, a reprint of a nineteenth-century Cloughton market byelaw, instructing that all farmcarts, hand- or horse-drawn, must stop at the weighbridge before goods were offered for sale. In Germanic fashion, all the nouns began with capitals. It had all made work for his predecessors, no doubt. Over the other side, similarly framed, was a picture entitled *The Vale of Plenty*. It showed a flat landscape, strewn with impressionistic apple trees and cornstacks. It had obviously been acquired from somewhere far removed from Cloughton. The title and the writing beneath were embellished with many scrolls. 'Meltsham and Evesham Farm Workers' Friendly Society', it announced. 'Established 1838 to tend the honest Labourer as he tends the Crops.' The honest labourer currently sitting beneath it was clad in a grubby anorak and a red bobble cap. He lit another cigarette from the stub of the last one and pushed his empty glass towards his companion who rose obediently to stand his round.

Twisting round to see what was hanging above his head, Browne drew in his breath. After a few seconds, he got up and reseated himself on Hunter's side of the table to look at the picture properly. It was of a slightly stylised owl, glaring balefully from its perch on a branch, proudly beautiful. It was painted without sentimentality but did not ignore the soft plumage and absurd markings which gave it the naive expression so beloved by the producers of those children's books that humanised wild creatures. It had the uncompromising ferocity of the hunting creature, concentrated and merciless, and yet Browne felt a foolish desire to reach out and stroke it.

He had always been fascinated by pictures, though he did not claim to be interested in art. Techniques and colours and concepts of balance and design excited him less than trying to fathom what it was about a particular object or scene that made a painter go to such pains to share with others what he had managed to see.

Hunter placed a cup of coffee in front of Browne and sat down beside him. 'What's this, then,' he asked, 'togetherness?'

Browne pointed to the picture that had caused him to change his place. Seeing his gesture, the landlord came over. 'It's got something, hasn't it, sir? My young nephew did it. There's some more of his stuff in the back if you want to come and look. He's only been using oils for a little while. The owl is the first thing that he's really been pleased with. He's painting in the back just now, seeing as you sent him home from school.'

'Does he live with you?'

'No, but I've got a spare room he uses for all his gear. He hasn't got the space at home.'

A thin, auburn-haired youth appeared from the nether regions and stood behind the bar. Browne recognised a rejected suitor of Virginia's, though it could be his version that he had grown tired of her.

'I've been telling the Inspector about you. This is my—'

Browne cut short the landlord's introduction and tried to alleviate the lad's embarrassment. 'Thanks, we have met. Hello, David. I didn't know you painted.'

The youth blushed deeper as they both looked towards his owl again. 'I'm only learning to. I used to work in watercolours because it was all I could afford but now I've got all this stuff from Mr Frayn.'

'Your uncle didn't tell me that.'

The boy took the ensuing silence as a sign of the Inspector's interest in his patron. 'Mr Watts, that's the art master, said something in the staff-room about my style needing the broader sweep of oils. Mr Frayn sent for me to talk about it.'

'He doesn't teach any art, does he?'

'No, but he's head of sixth form. We all talk to him about our work. He takes an interest in anybody who's good at anything. He'd seen my pictures before but I didn't know

I'd get on so much better in oils and neither did he.'

'So he bought you some oil paints and canvasses.'

'He said there was a fund for it and I could get a grant from school. I think he's the source of the fund, though, or why didn't Mr Watts tell me about it? He just got Mr Watts to order the things and, when he handed them over, said, "See if you can say anything with these, David." When I'd practised a bit, I did one that he liked. He bought it and said he was going to give it to Miss Bland on her birthday. Excuse me. I have to give my uncle a hand, washing the glasses.' He escaped from the embarrassing conversation before Browne could express his appreciation of the owl.

Hunter glanced at his watch, and by mutual consent, they made for the door. As they passed him, the honest labourer in the red cap spoke to them. 'I 'eard you and young David, on about Frayn. I 'aven't much time for most of 'em up at school but 'e's a good bloke. Took quite an interest in my youngster's running. Course 'e's left now, but Frayn used to turn out in the cold and wet to watch 'im race. Took 'im down to the local club an' found 'im a trainer there. Then, 'e marched 'isself round to our place and made me promise not to start 'im on this game.' He indicated his cigarette, drew on it, and turned back to his companions as the two policemen left.

To Browne's relief, Swann and Donaldson had finished their various horrible occupations in Miss Bland's study. He looked at their collection of sealed plastic bags and nodded to Swann. 'If you can just disturb the siesta that pair in the mortuary van are enjoying, we'll have the body moved and then we'll have our own look round.'

He returned to the office whilst two men with a stretcher bore off the body under the careful supervision of the Coroner's Officer. There he found Mitchell, hovering. He called through to the good-natured Swann. 'Care to give this young hopeful a running commentary whilst you pack away your stuff?' He closed the door on Swann's resignation and

71

Mitchell's delight and turned to find two steaming cups of coffee on the office desk.

'With the compliments of Mrs Barstow,' Hunter informed him. 'She thought we might as well benefit since she had to make it for "that lot".'

Browne tasted it and found it excellent. 'I fancy we're sampling Miss Bland's supply. I bet this isn't what they're drinking in the staff room.' He sank into the swivel chair and pushed the other cup towards Hunter. 'I don't think you were right, Jerry, about it being an unprofitable morning. In fact, you can earn your keep and tell me what we've learned about these people who are to provide our afternoon's entertainment.'

Hunter, who seemed unable to function, mentally, unless he was mobile, picked up his cup and drank from it whilst making circuits of the office. 'Right, sir. First there's Frayn. His behaviour this morning was peculiar, but, apparently, not untypical. If he's not guilty, he was unwise to visit the bathroom and remove his clothes. According to Maynard, he was at loggerheads with Miss Bland on the subjects of a Cambridge reference and the school play. According to his wife, there was also some disagreement about the school magazine. She thinks there was some affection for Miss Bland on her husband's part and a degree of dependence on Miss Bland's. This information was conveyed in an unconventional manner.'

Browne was impressed. 'Very concise. What about Freebourne?'

'She wasn't where she should have been at the relevant time. She has an interfering mother and a son who is no better than he should be. The latter was getting his deserts from Miss Bland, but could do no wrong in his mother's eyes.'

'Well, according to Mrs Barstow at any rate, though she doesn't see everything.'

'No,' Hunter agreed, dropping his official tone, 'she seems to have missed the juicy gossip about Miss Stafford. She has a pretty poor opinion of her. If she'd had any inkling of the alleged assault, she'd have enjoyed dropping at least some heavy hints. Stafford wasn't where she should have been at the time, either. I wonder what Miss Bland was intending to do about her.'

'And Mrs Weston?'

'She had the opportunity and she apparently brooks no interference in her office. That might be efficiency or it might be self-importance, but either way, it's useful if she has something to hide. I don't know what to make of the schizophrenic Maynard and we don't know much about the others.'

'Don't use medical terms you don't understand,' Browne admonished him. 'Otherwise, a very neat summing-up. You've earned that second cup of coffee.'

No further sounds could be heard from next door. Browne poked his head round to check. 'The lady's chamber is now at our disposal,' he announced.

'But,' Hunter reminded him, 'so are the long-suffering witnesses. They'll already be feeling pretty aggrieved at the indignities they've suffered. Hadn't we better see them?'

After a moment's thought, Browne shook his head. 'No, we'll go next door first. We might find something we need to ask questions about. And, by the way, I've had about as much of the larger-than-life Frayn as I can take at the moment, so, when we do see them, let's start with somebody else!'

Chapter 5

Miss Bland's office shared the colour scheme of the staff room with cheerful yellow walls and brown and yellow flowered curtains. A radiator ran the length of the wall under the window but it had done no harm to the healthy well-tended potted begonias on the sill. A long seating unit opposite the desk had plump foam cushions encased in brown tweed on each side of a shelf which held magazines. A locked metal filing cabinet stood in the corner, next to a cupboard which flanked the corridor door. A bookcase filled the space between the desk and the door connecting the office.

There were no pictures on the walls but the huge pinboard above the desk was well filled and colourful. A copy of the full school timetable took up about a third of it, a duplicate of the one Mrs Weston had consulted in the office. Bulldog clips were hooked to the frame, holding papers dealing with duty lists, fire drill procedures and similar routine matters. A small fan heater was tucked against the skirting board.

The room was functional, pleasant but impersonal, rather like the reception area in a hotel, except for the desk. It was of teak, topped with leather and man-sized. Browne thought that the small, dumpy woman who had sat at it must have looked out of place there. The swivel chair she had used was tweed-covered to match the rest of the upholstery. On the seat was a stain where blood had trickled along the arm and dripped from the elbow. On the floor, in front of the chair, drips from the desk had collected and soaked into the carpet, making a larger stain.

Free, now, to examine and touch as they pleased, Browne

and Hunter made a swift preliminary appraisal. 'Handbag first,' Hunter advised. 'It should provide the keys to open everything else.' He retrieved it from the shelf in the knee-hole of the desk. It was of good quality black leather, well used but polished and not shabby. He handed it to Browne who tipped out its contents on to the seating unit. Together, they surveyed them. A compact with a mirror, containing a disc of compressed cream powder and a clean velour puff, was the only item of make-up. The hoped-for keys were there, together with a house key on a separate ring, a fountain-pen, a comb and a red leather purse. The only interesting objects were a slim diary and a small bottle, clearly labelled, half full of tranquilliser tablets.

Browne replaced everything but the diary which he opened to the current week. According to the entries, Miss Bland had kept an appointment with her doctor last Saturday morning, had attended a meeting of her Parochial Church Council on Monday evening and had her hair done the night before. The current week mentioned no social engagements, but, turning the pages back Browne found reference to an invitation to supper with the Maynards and a theatre trip with 'J & K F', possibly the Frayns. He felt this surmise was confirmed when, over the page, in the forthcoming week, he found 'Geoff & Frances, Julian & Kate to dinner'. 'They won't be getting it now,' Hunter observed.

Browne nodded. 'I wonder what she had fixed for tonight.' He pointed to a capital B which was the only entry for that evening. All except one of the previous five weeks contained a similar entry, though not always on a Wednesday. Going further back, he discovered, in the second week in August, 'Met B at BM'.

'Woman friend? Man friend?' Hunter raised his eyebrows.

Browne shook his head. 'We shall see. I favour the latter suggestion. The hairdressing appointments faithfully precede these mysterious assignments, except the museum one. Let's move on for the moment.'

A small silver key on the official ring turned sweetly

75

in the lock of the grey filing cabinet which proved to contain copies of the education authority's ruling on all possible eventualities with the exception, probably, of this one. Hunter, who had been expecting staff files and personal records, was inclined to dismiss them. Browne, too thorough to pass anything over, but prepared to compromise, stuck his head into the corridor and beckoned Mitchell in.

Mitchell, after his interrogation and observation of the Scenes of Crime Officers, was inclined to be depressed.

'Did the wonders of science baffle you, then, Mitchell?' Hunter enquired.

Well aware that Hunter was not his greatest fan, nor an enthusiastic supporter of the accelerated promotion he hoped to enjoy, Mitchell replied, respectfully, 'No, sir, but I hope it's not going to make us redundant.'

Browne scowled at his protégé. 'What are you talking about, Mitchell?'

'Well, sir, by the time I've finished my training these labs will have done away with the need for studying human nature, getting people to reveal their motives and actions by skilful questioning.'

'If you want to study criminal psychology, Mitchell, go and get on with it, but don't come back for a job under me. In the meantime, I called you in to search this cabinet. Get busy.'

Browne turned back to the desk. On the left was a brown two-tone telephone and behind it two wire trays of correspondence. He swiftly checked though their contents. Across the front of the desk various papers were spread, blood-sprinkled and smudged except for the clean patch noticed first by Mitchell and another, almost as clean, where the cat had stood. This had presumably been removed by Donaldson.

Miss Bland's official school diary was lying open in one of the trays. Most of the jottings in it were unintelligible to Browne. He took '12.00 HOD' for Monday to indicate a lunch-time meeting with her heads of departments and 'Past Adv' on Tuesday morning had been, perhaps, a visit from the pastoral adviser from the education office. The school year and, therefore, the academic diary, began in September and so only six pages were written on. Tomorrow, there was to have been a governors' meeting, which someone would have to cancel or rearrange.

Seeing that Hunter had examined the head's small cloakroom and was moving on to the cupboard, Browne applied himself to the desk drawers, beginning on the right. The top one was shallow and merely contained boxes, neatly arranged, of drawing pins, paper clips, rubber bands and other office sundries. Below this, what appeared to be two drawers of equal depth was really one and contained the rack of personal files on the staff which Browne had been looking for. He took out those referring to the teachers awaiting his questioning and moved to the left-hand drawers. The top one contained a fair-sized polythene box. He removed the lid and blinked. Was this lunch for one or was she intending to throw a party? The drawer below contained what appeared to be sixth-form lesson notes. The bottom drawer was empty.

The three men briefly shared their findings. Mitchell reported that his filing cabinet contained only rulings from the education office. Hunter had found stationery in the cupboard, reference books in the bookcase and, in the small cloakroom, no sign that anyone had removed incriminating bloodstains from his person. Browne indicated the correspondence trays. 'Those seem to bear out the testimonials to her efficiency from Maynard,' he observed. 'No outstanding correspondence. Letters that arrived yesterday in the process of being answered. So, what have we discovered about her?'

'Not much from this room,' Hunter decided, 'though there's the bottle of Diazepam that backs up various people's suggestions that she was finding the job more than she could cope with.'

'And the lunch box,' Browne put in. 'She could have used the lunch hour to socialise with staff in the dining-room but she preferred to hide in here.'

'Maybe she was dieting. She was a fair-sized lady and school food is notoriously stodgy.'

Browne removed the plastic lid and displayed the gargantuan picnic: five or six slices of bread cut into dainty sandwiches, a pot of yoghurt, a cube of heavy fruit-cake, a wrapped chocolate biscuit and a banana. Hunter withdrew his suggestion and Mitchell hid his smirk.

'The most interesting question, so far,' Browne continued, 'is what was removed from this desk, presumably by the murderer. It was about the size of a foolscap envelope. I think we'd better find it. Meanwhile, Mitchell, there's work for you.' Mitchell straightened up eagerly. 'Grab your notebook and go along to the staff room to replace Bellamy. He'll have heard what they're all prepared to say to each other in front of a stranger. Having an old boy with his notebook at the ready might set their teeth on edge so that someone slips up. Keep your eyes open and, for once, don't try to merge into the background. Irritate them a bit – nothing against protocol, mind!' he added, as Mitchell grinned, mischievously.

He turned back to Hunter. 'I'll have a word with them all, Jerry, and then bring along the first victims. Whilst you're waiting, you might flip through that pile of staff files I've picked out and see if you find anything interesting.'

Browne and Mitchell left together and walked along the corridor in silence. Mitchell was wearing a worried expression and, as they neared the staff room, Browne paused, eyebrows raised. Recognising the invitation, Mitchell asked, hesitantly, 'Sir, I don't mind being teased about being a psychologist, or about anything else but do you agree with Sergeant Hunter that I'm going to mess up this scheme?'

Feeling it both pointless and dishonest to deny Hunter's animosity, Browne smiled at the for-once earnest young Constable. 'I wouldn't recommend you, Mitchell, if I didn't think you were the right material and the only way you might "mess it up" is by being too cocky. Be thankful for scientific evidence that keeps you on course. It's incontrovertible and that's why, in this force, we let it tell us all it will before we listen to the more subjective accounts of interviewees. The more available and more exact it becomes the better I like it, so learn to use it whilst you're working for me and don't foresee yourself as God's gift to coppers with the knack of getting all witnesses to eat out of your hand. And now we'd better go and appease these long-suffering ex-tutors of yours before they're so angry they won't answer any questions, yours, Hunter's or mine.'

The aforementioned company were variously disposed about the staff room, digesting the excellent meal prepared by Mrs Barstow, who might have despised its recipients but who valued her reputation as a cook. Her manner as she set it out had suggested that, whoever was guilty, they were all, with the exception of Maynard, equally deserving of being under suspicion. Her energetic disapproval, as she served them, was in marked contrast to the favours she bestowed on the blushing Bellamy. He hid his red face behind his notebook and made copious notes on the stilted conversation.

Their thoughts he had been unable to pin down. Sitting, knees crossed, in a corner, sipping instant coffee, Maynard wondered whether his wife had heard the news, and whether his strong urge to get in touch with her was so that he could reassure her, or she him. Beside him, Penny Stafford, head in hands, uttered a sound that was something between a sigh and a groan. He glanced at her, impatiently, and tried to feel some sympathy. It was possible that the girl was genuinely ill and she was certainly in a very worrying situation, professionally.

He let his mind wander over the indignities they had had to submit to at the police station and realised that he had quite enjoyed himself. He was probably the least well dressed of the staff who had been subjected to the humiliating procedures. Having his garments removed, one by one, to be placed in brown paper bags whilst he had stood on his brown paper sheet, it had occurred to him that his muscular, well-disciplined body would compare very favourably with what the removal of their smart, expensive garments revealed of his colleagues. He shuddered at the thought of an unclothed Miss Stafford.

Maynard thought that Kevin White, sitting opposite him, looked furious. He watched him drum his fingers on the table and thought he was probably composing letters to his MP and his union. He watched Meg Rivers as she rose from the other side of the room to refill her cup. She had too much sense to rail against the inevitable. She would have offered the police her full co-operation and allowed herself to feel no degradation. Frayn, who had been chatting to her, seemed to be enjoying himself. Trust Julian to find it all amusing. In the staff room, where she was not over-popular, Carol Weston seemed to have lost some of her smug composure. She had spent her time inspecting her nails and patting her hair and was now exchanging unenthusiastic remarks with Mrs Freebourne, who, as a lunch companion, was most people's last resort. It wasn't surprising, since her conversation centred obsessively on that objectionable son of hers whom everyone would so much rather forget. He was distracted from this long train of thought by the entrance of the Inspector.

Attention was riveted on Browne as he explained the afternoon's programme. 'Sergeant Hunter and I will see each of you in turn and I'm afraid that this surveillance will continue until that's over. Then you'll be free, except for any instructions Mr Maynard might wish to give you, provided we know where to contact you. Constable Bellamy and WPC Smith, who travelled up in the van with you, will be outside to accompany anyone who has to leave the room for any reason. I'll take Mr Maynard and Mrs Weston back with me and we'll make a start. I'll leave you with an old acquaintance, Detective Constable Mitchell.'

Wordlessly, Maynard and Mrs Weston followed him out, and Mitchell took Bellamy's seat in a silence compounded of anger and embarrassment. Having thought he was going to enjoy himself, Mitchell was surprised at how much their hostility disturbed him and how grateful he was for Frayn's broad wink.

Browne led his two witnesses first to Miss Bland's study. He held the door for Mrs Weston, who walked boldly past him and surveyed the scene coolly. Maynard followed and averted his eyes from the desk. 'I wanted to see you together,' Browne explained, 'because you were the two in the school who worked most closely with Miss Bland. Between you, I'm hoping you can tell me exactly what stage various matters had reached. But first I would be grateful if you'd both look round this room, very carefully, and tell me if anything is different from usual.'

They both looked round, obediently. When Mrs Weston's scrutiny reached the corridor door, she stopped. 'Her gown's missing from the hook on the door. She wasn't wearing it when we found her, was she?' She raised plucked brows at Maynard who shook his head.

Browne asked, suddenly, 'What are the rules about who does or doesn't wear a gown?'

Maynard turned back from his perusal of the notice-board and considered. 'There is no rule about it but, in practice, they're worn as a sort of badge of office by heads of department, senior teachers, deputies and so on. Actually there's a bit of bad feeling about it. This school was established as a comprehensive about fifteen years ago, formed from the old grammar school and the nearby secondary modern. Most of the hierarchy was chosen from the grammar school staff who were all accustomed to wear gowns for teaching and went on doing so. Last year, when the head of PE left and Kevin White was promoted, he borrowed mine and took all his games lessons in it on his first day, just to stir things up a bit.'

'How many people on the staff now customarily wear a gown?'

'Well, Mrs Rivers and Mrs Freebourne wear white overalls because of their work, even though they are HODs. Frayn only wears his when it's cold. Stafford doesn't.'

Browne noted that Maynard, usually punctiliously polite, had omitted to preface the last name with a title. 'I'd like you to tell me a little about Miss Stafford,' he said, 'but we might as well sit down first.' He opened the office door and ushered them through. Hunter stepped forward to place a chair for Mrs Weston, anticipating Maynard who got in his way. Maynard moved awkwardly out of it and pulled up a chair for himself.

Mrs Weston, who couldn't display herself to advantage on two fronts, decided to give Browne the benefit of the better view. 'What sort of thing do you want to know about Miss Stafford?' she asked him, shaking back the gleaming curtain of hair and preparing to enjoy herself.

Ignoring her, Browne turned to Maynard. 'Will you give me a brief account of the situation Miss Stafford had got herself into?' He went on as Maynard made a deprecating movement. 'We've seen some of the correspondence about it and we have to know. An objective version of it from you will do her less harm than a biased one from someone else.'

Mrs Weston shot him an aggrieved glance. Maynard sat back in his chair and thought about the matter, then, briefly, summarised the situation. 'She made a bad choice of career. She knows her subject but she doesn't know children. She can't keep order and she doesn't seem to want to make the effort to learn. Whenever a situation in school is difficult for her, she's unwell and has to go home.'

'You mean she pretends to be,' Carol Weston put in.

'Go on,' Browne invited, without turning his head from Maynard.

'The staff soon ran out of sympathy for her and she was foolish enough to confide her troubles in some of the sixth-form boys. She'd meet them in the pub and air her grievances to them. She's become a laughing stock. It's very worrying. Of course, some of the younger children have heard the older ones talking and, yesterday, a youth in her class passed a scandalous remark about her and his elder brother. He was insolent when she admonished him and she struck the child. He stumbled and cut his head on a desk. The whole room was in uproar.'

'Her classes always are.'

Browne quelled this interruption with a glare.

Maynard continued. 'Brenda and I came to see what

all the noise was about. Penny was in no state to teach. I sorted out the class and stayed with them till the end of the period and Brenda took Penny away to calm her down. The boy wasn't badly hurt and that would have been the end of it for the time being, except that Miss Bland wanted to consult me and couldn't raise me on the telephone in my office. She asked Mrs Weston to find me.'

This time, Mrs Weston was allowed to make a contribution. Browne turned to her enquiringly. 'Miss Bland was furious that Geoff had to waste his time like that. She's been worried for months because Stafford was an unhealthy influence. We ought to be rid of her. These are plenty of good teachers around.'

'And was Miss Bland thinking of getting rid of her?'

'She certainly wasn't prepared to hush everything up.'

'Was she encouraging the parents to make trouble for Miss Stafford?'

'She didn't have to. They were furious.'

Browne turned back to Maynard. 'Has Miss Stafford been involved in any other violent incidents?'

Maynard demurred. 'It wasn't a violent incident. The injury was purely an accident although Penny was unwise to resort to physical punishment. It's against the law now. When the child's mother arrived to collect him, Miss Bland was busy with another parent. I had the child in my office and reassured her that he'd come to no harm. We'd co-operated well in the past over her older boy and she'd calmed down by the time she left with the younger one. The senior staff thought, though, that the situation with respect to Miss Stafford had become serious enough to bring it before the governors and an extraordinary meeting had been arranged for tomorrow about it.'

'Did Miss Stafford know about this?'

'Not the details. Miss Bland sent her home yesterday – because she was upset, I mean. She hadn't suspended her. But she told her she would be getting in touch with the governors about the situation.'

'I see.' Browne nodded and caught Hunter's eye. 'I

wonder, Mrs Weston, if you would be kind enough to go back to the study with Sergeant Hunter and explain to him that baffling list of initials and notes in the official diary so that we can understand what Miss Bland's programme was.'

Hunter rose and Mrs Weston followed him out. With old-fashioned politeness, Maynard stood up as she left, then waited to see if he was dismissed. He was not.

'Just another minute or two, Mr Maynard. How would you describe your relationship with Miss Bland?'

Maynard did not like questions to which he could not give a precise and factual reply. His left hand returned to aggravate the wild disarray of his hair. There was a lengthy pause. 'Uneasy,' was the word he produced at last. 'I applied for the headship when she was appointed and she thought I resented her. I didn't. I was angry about it because I thought I'd have done a better job than she was doing. But I didn't blame her for being chosen.'

'Who did Miss Bland meet socially whose name began with B?' Browne asked suddenly.

Maynard looked baffled. 'One or two staff have that initial, but I thought the Frayns and my wife and I were the only staff who ever saw her out of school. Otherwise, I have no idea.'

'And, finally, will you tell me exactly what you did after you'd sent your two colleagues away from your office?'

Now he was being put on the spot himself, Maynard was relaxed again. 'That was just after ten to nine. I finished my coffee and thought about sorting out the mess in my office, but I decided to patrol the corridors instead. If there's an almost permanent staff presence out there it deters offenders.'

'Did you find any?'

'Yes, I despatched two smokers to assembly, after suitable retribution, of course, and watched them go.'

'Would you say there was any possibility that either of them perpetrated this attack?'

'Not those two. They wouldn't have had the time or the guts.'

'Thank you, Mr Maynard. That's all for now.'

He rose to go. Hunter had appeared in the doorway towards the end of this exchange. Browne winked at him. 'Where's the charming lady?'

'Asked to be excused. She's gone off with WPC Smith.' His eyes followed Maynard's retreating back. 'He's a fine one to say anyone else lacks guts.'

Browne's respect for the deputy had increased. 'I wouldn't underestimate Maynard. He may have the sensibilities of a Victorian maiden, but I think he'd stick by a moral judgment if it led him to a martyr's death.'

'He'd probably die it,' Hunter rejoined, 'a hundred times in anticipation.'

WPC Smith brought Mrs Weston back and she settled herself demurely, ankles neatly crossed. Browne examined his pen, minutely, as though suspecting it had some malfunction, then, looking sharply at her, asked, 'You don't like Mr Maynard very much, do you?'

She showed no surprise, merely answered the question. 'Not much.'

'Why is that?'

She glanced equally sharply at him. 'Does it matter who likes him? He wasn't killed.'

'True. Then did you like Miss Bland?'

'Well enough. We could work together. Aren't you going to ask me for any facts?'

The more Browne was irritated, the more urbane his manner became. 'Certainly I am. We'll deal with them at once if you're afraid you might forget them. What time did you arrive at school this morning?'

Angry colour stained Mrs Weston's cheeks, but she answered docilely enough. 'Twenty past eight as usual. I was working in this office by twenty-five past.'

'And then?'

'I put the coffee on, ready for Miss Bland's arrival.'

Browne swivelled his chair and looked through the window. 'You have a good view of this end of the car park. Did you happen to notice anyone else's arrival?'

She nodded. 'Yes, I keep an eye on who's coming in. Mr Maynard and I have to make arrangements for substitutes if anyone is absent so we both keep a mental check as we see the usual people turn up.'

'Excellent. And whom did you see?'

'Anne Scott, the lab technician, got here about five minutes after me and went through to the prep room.'

'You saw her go?'

'No, I just assumed she went there as usual. Then Miss Bland drove up at almost twenty to nine. I'd begun to think she wasn't coming.'

'Was it unusual for her to be late?'

'Definitely. It was the first time in nearly five years that she hadn't arrived immediately after me. She said she slept through her alarm.'

'After a late night, perhaps?'

Mrs Weston's mouth turned down at the corners to indicate the unsatisfactory nature of Miss Bland's social life. 'I know she was taking tablets for her nerves and sleeping pills too. She'd probably overdone it, although she didn't look as if she'd had a good night's sleep.'

'Did she appear abnormal in any other way?'

Mrs Weston thought about that. 'She didn't really have a normal. She was a bit moody, always different.'

'Not a good quality in a headmistress'

'Well, she had her problems.'

Browne abandoned his examination of his pen and slipped it in his pocket where he continued to finger it. 'Did Miss Bland come into the office to say good morning?'

'No, she went to her office through the corridor door. She'd raised her hand to me as she passed the window. I poured the coffee and took it through.'

'What did you talk about as you drank it?'

'We didn't. She was in a hurry and I had things to do. I put hers on the desk and came in here for mine.'

'So you don't know what she was doing after that?'

'Not exactly. The door was open and I heard her go into her cloakroom. Presumably she hung up her coat. I

86

heard the lavatory flush, then I heard her moving things on the desk. I thought she was writing something and then getting out the books she'd need for assembly.' She paused to rearrange the pleats of her skirt to her satisfaction. 'The registration bell went at ten to nine. As it stopped ringing, I saw Mrs Corby walk across the car park and towards the door.'

'That's Mrs Freebourne's mother?'

'Right. I heard her go into the biology lab across the corridor. Then Mr Frayn came into the office. It's past the date for giving me upper-sixth exam papers to duplicate but he only finished his last night. They're supposed to see to it themselves if they miss my deadline but he talked me into doing them and I thought I'd get on with it straight away before the day got any busier. I noticed that his pen had leaked on to his jacket pocket.' She looked at Browne, admonishingly. 'If you fiddle with yours any more, the same thing will happen to you.'

Hunter smiled as the Inspector obediently lowered his hand.

Mrs Weston went on, 'I've got some cleaning fluid so I made him take his jacket off till I had time to deal with it.'

'I gather you do at least like Mr Frayn.'

'He amuses me. He amuses everybody. It helps.'

Something in her tone suddenly made Browne see the staff from her point of view. They probably viewed her, constantly closeted with the head, with some suspicion and gave her as hard a time as she gave some of them. He smiled at her. 'Yes. He amuses me too. Did you leave the office together?'

She nodded.

'And by the corridor door?'

'Of course. The duplicating room's at the other side of Miss Bland's. I went in, set the machine up and switched on.'

'Did Mr Frayn go in to see Miss Bland?'

'No. It was time for the assembly bell. He went through the fire doors towards the hall.'

'In his shirt-sleeves?'

'I suppose he called in at the staff room to collect his gown.'

She started as Hunter put in a question from behind her. 'Who removed Miss Bland's empty coffee cup from her desk?'

'I did, as soon as I'd finished mine.'

'When?'

'After the registration bell and before Mr Frayn came in. It was when I got up to fetch it that I saw Mrs Corby.'

Browne shot an approving glance at his Sergeant and took over again. 'So Miss Bland was alive at eight fifty. How long did it take you to run off Mr Frayn's papers?'

Turning back to Browne made another adjustment of the skirt necessary. 'I can't tell you exactly, but when Geoff came in here, after assembly, I'd been back long enough to deal with Julian's coat.'

In the same manner as he had used to Maynard, Browne shot his question about the identity of B.

Mrs Weston looked interested now. 'I don't know. There's something, though. Last Tuesday, I took the school post to the main office as usual. When I looked in my handbag for the stamp money, I noticed my school keys weren't there and I remembered I'd left them on my desk. I'm not often so careless.'

Browne believed her.

'They'd probably have been safe. The caretaker would have picked them up. But I decided to come back for them. Miss Bland was still in her room, so I stuck my head round the door to say goodnight. She'd changed out of her school clothes and was wearing a dress that must have cost half a million and absolutely transformed her. I told her she looked positively alluring and she seemed pleased, but when I asked who merited a dress like that she bit my head off. I couldn't decide whether I'd been too familiar or whether I'd stumbled on her big secret. Anyway, I beat a hasty retreat.'

'That's interesting. Is there anything else that you know

and we've failed to ask about that you think would help us?'

She was silent for a moment. 'The cat. Was it the weapon?'

'We're making that assumption.'

'Well I can tell you about that. Miss Bland went up to London for a week or so during the summer. Her parents live there. She always visits the BM when she's there. She's keen on the Egyptians; shared their obsession with cats although she doesn't possess a live one. She got that model there. They're an exorbitant price, I believe. Everybody thought it was very attractive and picked it up to admire it. You'll find it has the fingerprints of half the staff on it.'

Browne thanked her and made his final request that she should set the duplicating machine going for them. Out in the corridor, the noise it made was slightly muted, but as it bounced and echoed on the hard surfaces of the tiled and plastered corridor, it was still sufficient to drown the screams of the fiends in hell. In sign language, Browne besought Mrs Weston to switch the machine off.

'This is a funny case, sir,' Hunter remarked as WPC Smith escorted Mrs Weston back to the staff room.

'They're all funny,' Browne growled. 'What's amusing you about this one?'

'Well, we've been handed on a plate all the information we usually spend ages searching for. If we accept Mrs Weston's evidence, we can pin down the time of the killing to between ten to nine and about ten or a quarter past when she switched the machine off. If it had happened after that, she'd hardly have failed to hear. And the weapon, too. It was still sitting gloating over its victim.'

'And do we accept Mrs Weston's evidence?'

'I don't know. We've only her word that Miss Bland was still alive at five to, and that she stayed with the machine all the time it was switched on. Why should she? I wouldn't stay, watching a machine drop papers in that infernal racket and those choking fumes. And she could have used the Head's cloakroom to wash and change, if necessary, though she's left no evidence there.'

'She does seem to be one of the few people here without an axe to grind against Miss Bland,' Browne ventured. 'Anyway, let's not be snapping on any handcuffs just yet. I've sent to see what Miss Stafford has to say.'

Chapter 6

There was a tap at the door, but it heralded the arrival, not of Miss Stafford but of Mrs Barstow bearing a tea tray. 'You'll need to wet your whistles after all them questions,' she informed them, 'and, if you've talked that Mrs Weston down, you deserve a cuppa. Good 'untin'.' Having deposited her offerings which included digestive biscuits and been suitably thanked, she breezed through the door, hips and hair bouncing, almost colliding with WPC Smith, whose arm, not very willingly offered, supported Miss Stafford. The cook's exuberant vitality emphasised Miss Stafford's self-absorption, and she certainly looked ill and shaken.

At a nod from Browne, Constable Smith stationed herself behind the chair which Hunter drew up and on to which Miss Stafford collapsed. Browne had seen her before at various school functions and had noticed the sallow pallor common to those who shun the outdoors, but her face was now alarmingly white. She slumped in the chair, a hand to her head, ignoring the other people in the room. Her posture announced that, since the Inspector wished it, she might as well suffer here as anywhere else. Hunter averted his eyes from the over-ample bosom, emphasised by the stretchy fabric in which it was encased. Browne tried to disregard the paranoid expression. WPC Smith stepped back and stood by the door; Hunter strolled behind the Inspector and looked out of the window.

Browne leaned forward. 'I'm sorry to have to bother you, Miss Stafford, when you aren't feeling well.'

She gave him a half smile, revealing buck teeth, a petulant

91

pink mouth and a weak jaw. 'I feel ghastly. I wasn't fit to come to school this morning. I wish I hadn't.'

'Well, since you did, I'll ask my questions as quickly as possible.'

Not much cheered by this prospect, Miss Stafford went on. 'I have the most dreadful migraines. I knew as soon as I woke up this morning that I was starting a particularly bad attack. By the time I got to school, I could hardly see.'

'You had no business to drive in that case,' Hunter admonished her over his shoulder.

Browne, who knew the symptoms of migraine on his own account, was sceptical. The pain of one of his attacks would not have encouraged him to describe his sufferings with such relish, nor would he have let the sunlight from the window play over his face as Miss Stafford was doing.

She showed Hunter a martyred resignation. 'My job is a responsible one and you have to learn to live with a recurring complaint, so I made the effort.' She waited for some sign that Hunter regretted his snub in the face of such altruism, then, disappointed, turned back to Browne.

'What time did you arrive at school this morning?' he asked her.

'I really couldn't tell you, Inspector. I had to drive more slowly than I usually do and if I'd looked at my watch, I'd only have seen flashing lights.'

Browne was unperturbed. 'Never mind, perhaps someone else will have noticed.'

Miss Stafford claimed Sue Rogers as a witness and re-counted that lady's kind assistance. 'She's new this term. New people have at least a term without a form.'

Browne nodded. Miss Rogers, he supposed, would learn not to be taken advantage of. 'So you were left alone in the staff room after the registration bell?'

'No, I wasn't. I might have been better off with my form than being upset by Kevin White's spitefulness.' Miss Stafford's performance was becoming less convincing as her irritation lent her face a little animation and colour. 'I wasn't going to listen to him. I was feeling dreadful and I knew I couldn't cope with my timetable. Wednesday is a very busy day for me. I came along to ask Miss Bland if I could go home.'

Browne sat up. 'You came along and spoke to Miss Bland after the registration bell?'

She protested violently. 'No! No! When I got to this end of the building, just by the dining-room I had to stop to be sick. I was leaning against the door, recovering a little, when Mrs Freebourne came in. She helped me to my car and said she'd let Mr Maynard and the Head know that I'd gone home. She offered to drive me but I didn't want to be a nuisance so she just popped my handbag on the passenger seat and told me to take care.'

'You had a handbag with you? Did it go to the police station when you did?'

Miss Stafford sat, immobile, pupils dilated.

'Constable Smith, would you please go home with Miss Stafford to fetch it?'

But Constable Smith only stooped to the floor where Miss Stafford had fallen, to loosen the collar of her sweater. They soon brought her round and after a few minutes, Browne considered Miss Stafford sufficiently recovered to be despatched with a police driver and Constable Smith as custodian-nurse to bring in the bag. Eager, in the meantime, for some conversation with a fit and cheerful human being, he plumped for Mr White and summoned him.

As they waited, Browne divulged to Hunter what they already knew about him. 'Mitchell chanced to remark this morning, whilst reminiscing about his illustrious school career, that people usually do what Mr White wants.'

Hunter scowled. 'If Mitchell did, then White's a formidable character.'

Ignoring this jibe, Browne continued, 'Sergeant Tuckey tells me that whilst his colleagues were kicking their heels and waiting to get their clothes back, White redeemed the time by doing close on a hundred press-ups.'

'Remarkable.' But the flat tone showed that Hunter was unimpressed.

Kevin White, when he entered, proved to be what Browne had heard described as a clean-cut young man. He was on the tall side of middle height, lean and healthy-looking. His crisp dark hair was cut sufficiently short for the wild cross-football-pitch winds not to disarrange it and his dark eyes met the Inspector's, mutually appraising. He settled himself on the chair that Browne indicated and began the proceedings himself.

'I'd better tell you before anyone else does that I made an unfortunate remark in the staff room this morning.'

'Is that so?' Browne suddenly remembered that Virginia was smitten with this young man. He appeared in photographs adorning her bedroom wall, surrounded by members of his various teams, whom, she hoped, would divert her parents' suspicions. He returned his attention to the matter in hand. 'Unfortunate for whom?'

'For me and possibly also for Miss Bland.' He explained the circumstances which had caused his annoyance.

'And your remark was?'

'I said someone would do the old bat in if she went on provoking us. I also said that the model cat would make a handy weapon.'

'I see. And you think that you put the idea into someone's head?'

'It looks like it. Or do you suspect a double bluff?' His tone registered no alarm, however.

Browne watched him. 'Can you remember who was in the staff room at the time?'

'Just about everybody. They were all waiting for the registration bell. I was waiting for my favourite moment of the day.' Browne's eyebrows invited an explanation. 'When they all dash off to mark registers and Sue and I, who haven't got forms, pour ourselves another cup of tea. But today, she was playing angel of mercy and I had Stafford for company. You've spoken to Penny Dreadful, haven't you? I expect she told you I was a prophet of doom.'

Browne refused to be drawn. 'She told me you were unkind to her.'

White grinned. 'It was Julian. I only laughed. She came in as she does about once a week, miming the symptoms of the last stages of a wasting disease. Julian said he didn't know which complaint she was attempting so he wasn't sure what to award for technical merit, but he'd give her the full six for artistic impression.'

Hunter gave a short laugh and White seemed to notice him for the first time.

Browne bit his lip. 'Perhaps you'll help me get a few facts straight now. What time did you arrive at school this morning?'

'I couldn't say exactly. About twenty to nine. Several of us were held up by a badly parked dust-cart and Frayn walked across the road just as we left the car park. We all hung our coats in the appropriate places and went to the staff room.'

'Where you stayed till the end of assembly?'

'No. After a bit I'd had about as much of Stafford as I could stand, sighing and groaning and guzzling tea. I'd read the sports pages in the staff room papers by then and I was thinking of matches nearer to home. We've got one at four o'clock against – oh, Lord, I'd better ring up and cancel it as soon as you've finished with me.'

'Write the number and details down and someone will do it for you now.' Browne tore a sheet from his notebook. White scribbled and passed it to Hunter who handed it with muttered instructions to a constable outside.

'Go on.'

'I was a bit worried about the pitch. I thought I'd look at it before first lesson started.'

'What time did you leave the staff room?'

White shook his head. 'It was after Julian had nipped home. A few minutes past nine.'

Brown blinked and began fiddling with his pen again. 'I'll come back to that. So you and Miss Stafford were together until about five past nine?'

White shook his head. 'No. She kept nipping out.'

'For unspecified purposes?'

White snorted. 'They were specified only too clearly, heave by disgusting heave. But I didn't believe her then. She said she was too ill to stay and she was going home. I said she'd better report to the office first.'

Browne changed tack. 'How did you know that Mr Frayn had gone home?'

'I saw him through the window. He crossed the road just after the hymn finished.'

'Can you remember what he was wearing? It's important.'

White obligingly gave the matter his full attention. 'Light flannels and his gown, I think.'

'And you're sure the hymn had finished? Do the children sing loudly enough to be heard in the staff room?'

'No, but Barry plays the organ loudly enough to be heard in the town hall.'

'I see. There's only one more point. Which way did you go to and from the games field?'

He answered promptly. 'I went out through the old foyer and round the new block. I came back through the admin block and along the bottom corridor.'

'Past Miss Bland's room?'

White nodded.

'Did you see anyone either way?'

'On the way there not a soul. On the way back, I saw old Barstow with his mop and bucket, cleaning up after Penny Dreadful. I saw Mrs Freebourne outside with her by the car. I made her a mental apology. She hadn't looked ill in the staff room and I'd been sure she was putting it on.'

Browne dismissed him and let him go to the door before asking, 'Do you know anyone Miss Bland was friendly with whose name begins with B?'

White shook his head. 'I seldom noticed her being civil to anyone, never mind friendly.'

'So everyone does as White wants,' Hunter reflected as the door closed behind him. 'Miss Bland apparently didn't. He obviously didn't like that very much.'

* * *

96

There was a tap on the door and Constable Smith appeared, having deposited her charge on one of the corridor chairs. Taking it from her, Browne upended his second handbag of the day on to the tweed cushions. Like the first it contained purse and keys, but there was no diary and the make-up items were more extensive and elaborate, zipped into a flowered nylon bag. Hunter picked up three small bottles and read the labels. 'Ye gods, is everybody in this place on tranquillisers?' he demanded.

'Teaching is a hard life, Jerry,' his superior told him and he was unable to assess the irony in the statement.

Browne unzipped a side pocket and reached gingerly inside. Finding what he expected, he felt for a pair of tweezers in his pocket and used them to extract the stained brown foolscap envelope. He laid it on the desk, and, holding it with the tweezers, slit it open with Miss Bland's dainty paper-knife. He drew out the folded sheet it contained, being careful not to finger it, and held it in the top corner with the tweezers to read it through.

After a few seconds' silence, Hunter grew impatient. 'Is it curtains for La Stafford?'

His expression inscrutable, Browne read aloud, 'Dear Mr Bingham, After careful consideration, I have decided that I must tender the governors my resignation from the post of headmistress of Heath Lees School.' Quickly, Hunter came round the desk and they examined the letter together. It was brief and offered no specific reasons for Miss Bland's decision, saying merely that she had come to the conclusion that the appointment had been a mistake.

'Presumably,' Hunter volunteered, 'Miss Stafford thinks, as we did, that this letter concerns her.'

Browne nodded. 'We won't disillusion her for the moment.' He scooped Miss Stafford's possessions back into her handbag, after placing the letter and envelope in a sealed plastic bag. He crossed to the window and looked out. He did not relish a continuation of his interview with Miss Stafford. Hypochondria had always profoundly irritated him, and the courteous bullying of the

97

inadequate personality awaiting him seemed a distasteful way to spend the rest of the afternoon. In fact he was feeling a profound dislike of the whole case. Having his key witnesses banished for the whole morning seemed to have hobbled the investigation, in spite of his assertion to the contrary to Hunter, though he acknowledged that, since he had given the orders for it himself, the feeling was unreasonable.

Mrs Barstow, walking down the road, a shopping bag over her arm, her brassy hair bobbing, crossed his line of vision. She caught his eye, gave him a broad wink and mimed that there would be more refreshment provided on her return. He raised a hand to her, cheered to an irrational degree by her ebullience rather than the promise of tea. He turned and nodded to Hunter to invite Miss Stafford back in.

She entered and stared at him for a second, before sinking on to her chair and closing her eyes. Ignoring these histrionics, Browne spoke severely. 'Miss Stafford, you have wasted our time and lied to us. We know, now, that when you came to this corridor this morning you entered Miss Bland's office and removed an envelope from her desk. We are conducting a murder enquiry, and if you refuse to tell us the truth, we can only draw our own conclusions about the reasons for it. Now, would you like to try again?'

It seemed Miss Stafford had prepared herself for the rebuke. In a barely audible voice, but composedly, she retold her story. 'I came here at about nine o'clock to say I had to go home. I knocked on the office door and went straight in. We always do.'

'That's better. Go on.'

'Mrs Weston wasn't there, and I realised I could hear her working in the duplicating room. My head was pounding so hard that, although the noise made it worse, I hadn't really registered it before.'

Browne firmly ignored his impulse to shake her and let her continue.

'The door to Miss Bland's room was slightly open. I thought she was in assembly, but I tapped and peeped round the door to be sure.' She closed her eyes again. 'I saw her.' Miss Stafford swallowed, then gathered herself and went on. 'There was blood all over her and she had a surprised look on her face. I thought I was going to faint and I held on to the door and closed my eyes. When I opened them, I found I was staring at an envelope on the desk, addressed to the governors.'

'Which you know we have found in your bag.'

She leaned back in her chair and closed her eyes again. Browne wondered if the interview would proceed any more quickly if he offered her a blindfold. Without opening them, she asked for a glass of water and Browne strove to control his impatience whilst Constable Smith provided it. He allowed her one sip before renewing his attack.

'Why did you take it?'

She took a further long drink, then handed the glass back to Constable Smith. Her voice rose, petulantly. 'Because she was trying to get rid of me. She didn't like me and she was trying to turn a little incident into a major crisis. No one else was taking that attitude. Mr Maynard and Mrs Viner were quite reasonable. With her out of the way and the letter out of the way, I'd have been all right.'

Hunter looked up sharply to find Browne glaring at him, and hastily lowered his eyes. Browne calmly continued the interrogation.

'Let's go back to the beginning, shall we? I'll tell you what we already know and you can fill in what's missing. Mr Maynard told me that there was an unfortunate incident in one of your lessons yesterday. A boy was injured because you hit him and he was caught off balance. He'd annoyed you because of something he'd said, a piece of childish silliness.'

This merciful euphemism was wasted and both policemen were startled by the viciousness of the woman's outburst. 'The little rat suggested that I'd invited his older brother to sleep at my flat! Some of the things he's been saying have been repeated to other members of staff. Mr Wonderful Frayn dared to say to me yesterday that I'd have to behave

99

more discreetly with some of the sixth-form if I didn't want to find myself in worse trouble. And for him of all people to dare to say such things!'

'Are you suggesting that his own conduct is not above reproach?'

She glared at them, angrily. 'What do you think? His wife's young enough to be his daughter and the way he fusses over the Kelsey girl is disgusting.' Suddenly, she smiled. 'By the way, when I was coming to the office to see Miss Bland, I passed him coming the other way.'

Browne's reaction evidently disappointed her. 'Yes, we know about that. Let's get back to the relevant facts, shall we? You think Mr Frayn was against you as well as Miss Bland in this matter?'

'He was but he couldn't do anything about it. The silly old poseur doesn't have as much influence as he thinks he does. Mr Maynard was the one who'd spoken to the brat's mother and he'd smoothed things over. Only Miss Bland wanted to stir things up, writing to the governors. She didn't waste much time, did she?'

'When you went into Miss Bland's office, Miss Stafford, did you notice whether her gown was hanging in its usual place behind the door?'

'I was too upset to notice anything.' Ready tears welled under the heavy lids.

Watching her grope for a handkerchief, Browne could suddenly take no more. 'We may need to see you again, Miss Stafford, but that will do for the moment.'

When she had gone, he endeavoured to ignore his contempt and view her evidence objectively.

Hunter had no such compunction. 'What an object!' was his comment as he exercised his freedom to ride his chair again, pressing his chest against its back. 'In our man's place, I'd have used my murderous energy to despatch that one and let Miss Bland off for a bit longer.'

Browne's thoughts were running along a different track. 'I wonder if anyone shares her opinion that not all Mr Frayn's relationships are quite healthy. I think we've had him on ice long enough, now, Jerry. The longer he's corked up, the more he'll bubble and fizz.'

Julian Frayn, when he appeared, confirmed all Browne's forebodings that the extraction of basic facts could be a slow process.

'I've been trying to decide,' he remarked, pleasantly as he made himself comfortable on his chair, 'whether incarceration in my monkish cell was a deterrent or a therapy.'

Browne decided it would be easier and probably more productive to give him his head. 'And did you manage to come to any conclusion?'

Frayn shook his head. 'Not really, but I've quite enjoyed myself. We're always lecturing our charges about continuing their education beyond school and I had my experience enlarged this morning in quite an unexpected direction.'

'I'd like you to describe your experiences earlier this morning.'

Frayn's bright brown eyes met the Inspector's. 'You mean, give an account of my movements at the relevant time?'

'That's right.'

'Where shall I begin?'

'With your arrival at school.'

'Oh, splendid. Then I needn't give details of my unchivalrous remarks to my wife over breakfast.'

'We have them, already.'

Frayn contorted his features into a lugubrious expression. 'I assure you, Inspector, that Kate will loyally have whitewashed my share in the proceedings. I behaved abominably.'

'No doubt. It doesn't interest me for the moment. What time did you arrive at school?'

'About eight thirty-five. I spoke to a pupil in the foyer, then spent a little time marking and drinking tea.'

'So nothing of any moment occurred before registration?'

'Indeed, it did, Inspector. A prophecy was uttered by Mr White. He has assured us since that it was his first and

101

his last, but as befitted this only manifestation of his augural competence, its fulfilment was imminent and accurate.'

'We know about that, too.' Frayn's prosiness did not annoy Browne but it amused him to become monosyllabic in inverse ratio to it. 'Go on.'

'Not appreciating the significance of Kevin's remark, we ignored it. The registration bell rang and we departed to discover which of our charges had deigned to check in for the day's entertainment.'

Browne reflected that this was probably a fair description of what Frayn's charges received. He contemplated the man facing him. Tall and spare, Frayn was probably in his early fifties. His hair was thinning and greying though he had no bald patches. The face was lined but it still more than adequately transmitted the alert mind and powerful personality. Not in the least disconcerted, Frayn returned the scrutiny as he waited for his catechism to continue.

'Your business with your form was soon dealt with.'

Frayn agreed. 'I told them to go down by themselves when the assembly bell rang. They are upper sixth-formers, after all. I had to try to charm Mrs Weston into duplicating my exam questions which were well overdue. She was in an obliging mood. Not only did she agree to do them then and there but, after a mild lecture on my messy appearance, she confiscated my jacket to remove an ink stain from the pocket. I hadn't even noticed it. Then I went to assembly.'

'Did you visit Miss Bland for any reason before you left?'

'What, in my shirt-sleeves? She highly disapproved of *déshabille* about the school. I nipped off for my gown and went to the hall.' Anticipating the next question, he added, 'It was in my form room. I had to pass it on the way.'

'Did you meet anyone?'

He grinned. 'Yes, coming out of my form room, I spied the dying swan. She was walking quite briskly until she saw me, after which she adopted a convincing droop.'

'You're talking about Miss Stafford?'

'You obviously recognise the description.'

'Why did you leave assembly before it was over?'

Frayn displayed amusement as Browne waited for his answer. 'For a variety of reasons. The hall was cold and I hadn't my jacket on. I found myself standing next to Miss James, the PE woman. Empty-headed, steel-muscled women irritate me and this one was singing, lustily but off-key, down my left ear. The words she was bawling suddenly registered. "The Lord gave Him my form to take." I managed to smother my laughter until I was out of the door and had space to ask myself whether the compiler of the hymn book was too slow-witted to see the joke, or whether the *double-entendre* made him include it in a school hymnal to amuse such worshippers as were awake enough to realise what they were singing.'

Browne was finding himself hugely entertained, his frustration and impatience of half an hour ago quite dissipated. 'So you decided to go home?'

'Well, I fell to imagining what it would be like to be married to Pat James, and then I couldn't wait to offer Kate a humble apology.'

With a twinkle in his eye, Browne produced what had become this afternoon's refrain, 'Yes, we know about that.' Nevertheless, he took Frayn meticulously through the hour or so he had spent away from the school. 'Do you make a habit of this sort of thing?' he asked finally.

Now, Frayn returned the twinkle. 'If you mean did I buy a house so conveniently near school so that I could spend my free periods availing myself of my conjugal privileges, the answer is no. I do go home occasionally in my free time if the staff room conversation drops to the level of last night's ration of the current soap opera, but usually I spend it trying to diminish my mountain of marking. It's a bind but I can hardly ask my pupils to take their work seriously if I don't devote time to what they write.'

'I have reason to believe that your pupils take their work very seriously.'

'I'm pleased to hear it. I hope your source of information was your daughter. There's no gainsaying satisfied customers.'

'You'll be glad to hear you've received an accolade.'

'I'm not sure that I deserve it. I transmit factual knowledge and a few ideas in an entertaining fashion. My pupils remember being amused and, occasionally, the substance of what diverted them, but most of them don't discipline themselves to learn. I can't persuade them to that. For the most part, I fit flabby minds with mental corsets. Most of them make little significant use of what they learn beyond reproducing it on a piece of paper in order to be awarded another piece which they wave at prospective employers.'

His face did not express the disillusion of his words. It was lit up with a fanatic's enthusiasm. Browne prompted him. 'But there's more than that in it for you.'

'That's right. In each school year we get half a dozen or so children who justify my existence. Of course they'd pick up the knowledge they need without my help, but at least I can save them some time, point them to the right books, challenge their ideas so that they are forced to examine their own potential.'

'Is Valerie Kelsey one of her year's half-dozen?' He saw that he had helped Frayn up on to his hobby horse.

'She and another pupil in her year, David Draper, are the most talented children the school has contained since I came here fourteen years ago.'

Browne said, 'Yes, I know David. I was admiring his owl in the pub at lunch-time.'

'It's quite exceptional, isn't it? There's not much we can give him here. He has what he needs within his own vision so long as someone provides him with his raw materials.' Browne did not embarrass Frayn with references to his own generosity on this count but let him continue. 'He's only done two oil paintings apart from a few practice daubs. The other is of poppies in all their glory on a bit of waste ground in an industrial scene. When he'd finished it, I bought it and, on impulse gave it to Sarah as a birthday present.'

'And Valerie? I understand there was some disagreement between you and Miss Bland about her reference.'

'That's right. Usually, I write sixth-form references and

Miss Bland countersigns them, but she wouldn't pass the one I wrote for Valerie.'

'Because of what you didn't say? Do you really think the girl's record can be brushed under the carpet and forgotten? If she's such a good candidate, why does she need to get in on false pretences?'

Frayn sighed angrily. 'The circumstances that would be pleaded in mitigation wouldn't sound so bad on paper as they must have been for a girl of her type to live through. Cambridge can weed out any people who seem to them undesirable on any count and still have hundreds of high calibre candidates left to choose from. They might have rejected her without realising what she was offering them. I just wanted the bad record kept back until they'd met her, seen some of her work. But the head was obdurate. She couldn't have the school blamed when it all came out later.' Frayn mimicked the head's tones bitterly. 'She and I both talked about the good of the school but we meant different things by it. She meant its reputation, and by that her own. I meant what was best for every child who passed through our hands.'

'Would Valerie not have done just as well at one of the redbricks?'

Frayn looked exasperated. He had obviously been asked this question before. 'Cambridge still attracts the best teaching that's available; the calibre of student stimulation is much higher, and the bit of paper they give is still worth more than any other university's if she goes on in academic circles. Valerie has a fine mind that deserves the atmosphere and resources there.'

It occurred to Browne that the world that would appreciate that fine mind, trained in that particular fashion, had passed away. He did not think there was a great deal of point in expressing that view to Frayn. He change the subject slightly. 'Apart from this controversy, how did you get on with Miss Bland? Did you dislike her?'

'On the contrary, in some ways I liked her very much. In practical matters she was quite relaxed and forthcoming.

Some of the staff here wouldn't have recognised her as a hostess to people she felt at ease with. She was an inspired cook.'

'She offered you hospitality?'

'She didn't entertain much, but if she invited people, Kate and I were usually included. The conversation wasn't up to the standard of the food, though she liked to consider herself a very well-read lady. There wasn't a book written that she hadn't read a review of.'

Browne winced. 'Is your criticism of your pupils so devastating?'

Frayn smiled. 'I temper it to what they can understand and what they can bear.' Seeming to consider this a good exit line, Frayn rose to leave.

'One more question please.'

Frayn paused politely.

'You seem to have been as much in Miss Bland's confidence as anyone. Her diary refers to various assignations with a person she refers to as B. Can you elucidate?'

He hesitated a fraction too long, then said, 'So Kate was right. No, Inspector, I can't give you a name, but Kate thought there was a man somewhere in the picture, recently. Like Mamillius, she "learned it out of women's faces" – or Sarah's in this case.' Seeing Browne's puzzlement, he laughed. 'I'm sorry, Inspector. My acquaintance with detectives before today has only been in fiction. Alleyn and Wexford and Dalgleish quote Shakespeare oftener than the rule book. I must remember that you are flesh and blood. It's from *A Winter's Tale*. Ask Virginia. It's her set book. Or, better still, come and see our production. It can go ahead now that Miss Bland's objections are removed.'

And, on this line, he did manage his grand exit.

Hunter immediately resumed his peregrinations. 'Do they all want us to clap the handcuffs on them?' he demanded. 'Frayn departs, rejoicing that Miss Bland's death removes all obstacles to his forthcoming play. Miss Stafford assures us that now she's out of the way everyone will be prepared to forget her own little peccadilloes.' He realised the Inspector was deep in thought. 'What are you thinking about?' he asked.

Browne ticked off the questions on his fingers. 'First, I'm wondering what relationship Miss Bland had with B, and why Frayn automatically assumed it was a man.'

'Well, you did refer to assignations.'

'True. Then, I'd like to know why Miss Stafford was pretending to be suffering from a migraine attack.'

'How do you know she was?'

'She got some of the details wrong.'

'But she did seem ill.'

'She was certainly genuinely upset just after nine o'clock, but that was after viewing the bloody remains.'

'Or after beating them over the head to get back what she thought was a letter that sealed her fate.'

'True again.'

'And what about White, sir? It was strange that he prophesied the event so accurately.'

Browne made a final note in his book. 'I think we shall have to follow him up a bit further. Where was he trying to plant his idea?'

Chapter 7

For his interview with Mrs Freebourne, Browne decided he needed a change of scene. As the afternoon progressed, he was finding the small office progressively more claustrophobic and the investigation more tedious. He felt an urge to make physical inroads on the case, to rush about making things happen, but he knew that his primary duty at this stage was to hear and compare the evidence of all the available witnesses. He wondered if this was the feeling that made Hunter so restless that he had to prowl in circles except when he was actually asking questions or taking notes. In addition, it seemed more sensible to question the biology mistress in the place where she had spent the crucial time.

He walked to the front of the lab and stepped on to the raised dais between the blackboard and the teacher's bench from where Mrs Freebourne had been giving her lesson during first period. He examined, apparently idly, a pile of exercise books, a box of biro pens and a bunsen burner with its rubber tubing perished at one end. An envelope, containing notes on single-cell life lay on top of a half-empty box of man-size tissues. Browne stood up from the desk and grimaced at the mess of greasy chalk dust on his sleeve. As he tried to brush it off, he viewed the wearing of gowns for teaching in a new light. They might provide good protection against the draughts in this room, too.

Stepping off the dais and wandering to the middle of the room, he surveyed it from there. The blackboard informed anyone who might be interested that, 'The expelling of undigested food is not EXCRETION but EGESTION.'

Being a man who liked his terminology to be accurate, Browne made a mental note. He turned to look through the window behind him. Since the lab lay on the opposite side of the corridor from the office and the Head's study, Browne had presumed himself to be still on the ground floor, but the slope of the land had left scope for a storage room underneath. He was looking out over its projecting tarred felt roof, patterned with moss and the marks of dried-up puddles. Two abandoned tennis balls nestled together in the gutter beside a piece of unpolished wood of a shape which suggested no possible use. Nearer the window were several sweet wrappers and a rusty pair of compasses, dropped through the window by bored and unaspiring embryo biologists.

Turning back to the room, he contemplated the skeleton in the front corner, packed with plastic replicas of its once vital organs. Its skull leered mockingly at the two policemen. On a childish impulse, Browne stuck out his tongue at it, then joined Hunter, who was examining with approval a display of pupils' posters under a paper banner which announced 'NO SMOKING' in huge red capitals. The quality of the work varied considerably, but the artists had been well furnished with information. A sheet emblazoned with 'No Somking' caused Browne a prickle of irritation. If the woman couldn't impose correctly spelt terminology on her charges, surely she didn't have to display the fact. He noted with surprise the name in the bottom corner, 'Neville Freebourne'. Another effort on the top row dissipated his irritation. It showed Mitchell, cleverly caricatured, hand-cuffed to a shopkeeper who was handing cigarettes over the counter to a small boy. Browne could not decide whether the latter's resemblance to Hunter's young son was coincidental, but he felt reasonably certain that this was another example of David Draper's work.

He pointed it out to Hunter. 'Oh, it's deliberate all right,' Hunter assured him. 'Draper came round a couple of weeks ago to do a pencil sketch of Tim and to ask me if I minded if he used it for this. I was amused; so was Tim.'

109

Their admiration of the cartoon drawing was cut short by the arrival of Constable Smith with Mrs Freebourne. She stood nervously near the door, looking towards her usual refuge behind the bench as though she could function from that place only. Browne saw a tallish, thin woman, smartly dressed in a suit and crisp cotton blouse. She had taken considerable trouble to lift and curl the wispy fair hair into an illusion of greater abundance and the make-up was clever and restrained.

'We're just admiring Draper's poster,' he remarked, and she came to join them in front of the display.

'We ran a competition,' she explained, 'for different age groups.'

'And these are the winning entries?' Hunter was unable to keep the surprise from his voice or his eyes from Neville Freebourne's careless and unremarkable entry.

She flushed and smiled with her mouth. 'Nev's spelling's awful. I can't do anything with it and it looks as if the English staff can't either, but his science is sound enough.'

Browne let this pass. 'I asked you to come here to make it easier to explain what you were doing. Will you please take us through your movements from your arrival at school?' He took her quickly through the staff room chat, the registration of her form and her attention to the bees and locusts, and her answers produced no surprises. He pressed on. 'I understand your mother visited you here this morning.'

She flushed and answered awkwardly, 'I'm afraid she did.'

Browne waited for this remark to be elaborated. When it wasn't, he asked, 'Were you surprised to see her? Does she normally come into school?'

Mrs Freebourne fidgeted on her stool. 'She's wandered in a couple of times. I wouldn't say it had become a habit yet.'

'What did she want?'

She sighed and sat contemplating a minute chip in her pale pink nail varnish. Before she broke the silence, she looked up and directly at him. The eyes were unfaded blue, black-fringed. It occurred to Browne that she must once have been very attractive. 'In the short term, she wanted me to know that she had seen my daughter, Melanie, in what she considered undesirable company. In the long term, she wanted me to go home and be a domesticated little housewife, privileged to receive daily visits from her for instructions on how to run the house, how to dress and bring up my children, and when to breathe in and out.'

Half sympathetically, half fearing that he was opening the floodgates, Browne asked, 'Is she a widow?'

'No, she isn't, but she's so cowed my father that domineering over him doesn't use up much of her energy any more. I used to be just as much under her thumb. When she sent me to university, it never occurred to her that it would change me. She just thought it would put her one up on the neighbours. My degree would be a badge of her first-class motherhood, but she didn't expect it to lead to work outside the home and hobbies that aren't domestic, or leaving my children free to develop their own interests and make their own decisions. She calls it letting them run wild.'

Browne saw that Glenys Freebourne could talk on this theme all day. He cut in, politely, his question relevant. 'Was she so concerned about your daughter's "wildness" that she couldn't put off talking to you till you were at home?'

'I doubt it, but she insists on the fiction that my husband has forbidden her the house.'

'But he hasn't?'

'He only told her he wouldn't have his family insulted in their own home so she'd better wait to visit us until she had something pleasant to say to us. If she wanted to come she'd ignore anyone's forbidding, but she's just a little afraid of Ted; she'd rather tackle me when I'm alone, and she can count the supposed banishment as another grievance.'

'What time did she arrive here?'

'About ten to nine.'

'And left?'

'About ten past.'

'Were you together for the whole of those twenty minutes?'

She nodded.

'And then she went home?'

'I expect so. I had to get rid of her before assembly finished. I told her I'd have a word with Melanie and went outside to see her off. She was still muttering.'

'I think you met Miss Stafford whilst you were outside.'

'Yes, I did.' Diverted from her own troubles, Mrs Freebourne became less intense. 'I felt rather guilty. I didn't have much patience with her earlier. We all thought she was just making a bid for sympathy and attention and I joined in Julian's teasing by laughing. But when I came back in she looked ghastly and she was certainly very sick. I wanted to drive her home, but she insisted, almost hysterically, that she'd rather drive herself, so I let her. It was only about a mile. She overtook my mother at the gate as I watched. My mother will make a good witness for you. She misses nothing, whether it's her business or not.'

Browne was saved from a return to her relations with Mrs Corby by a knock at the door, followed by the entrance of Bellamy and two youths. One of them, small, slight and grimy, grinned nervously round, obviously feeling a mixture of excitement and alarm at having penetrated to the heart of the investigation. The other boy, fatter and sulkier, lumbered behind him, and one glance at Glenys Freebourne's stricken face told Browne that here was Neville. He regarded the boy grimly, repressing a double urge to rip out his gold earring and put him on a strict diet. Both boys wore uniform now somewhat the worse for wear and the front of Neville's shirt was heavily stained with blood. Bellamy indicated that both boys should seat themselves on lab stools. Then he fished a handkerchief from his pocket and, wrapping it round his fingers, proceeded to pinch the fleshy middle of Neville's nose.

Continuing his ministrations with an ungentle touch, Bellamy spoke over his shoulder. 'These two are Kevin Stocks and Neville Freebourne, sir. Freebourne was found by Dean trying to effect an entry by the storage room window below this room. Dean told him he wasn't allowed in and he demanded to see his mother.' Bellamy dropped his official tone and chuckled. 'He claimed that this young whippersnapper had walloped him. I went out when I heard all the commotion and spotted Stocks. He didn't take much catching.'

'It's time someone caught up with him.' Mrs Freebourne was white-lipped and furious. 'Inspector, this is the second time this boy has assaulted my son. I'm making an official complaint.'

Stocks, who had shown much offence at Bellamy's term of reference, now turned to his accuser, losing six inches of height by sliding off the high stool and standing on his own two feet. ' 'E shouldn't throw stones at my dog, then. If 'e does it again, I'll make a 'ficial complaint to t'animal welfare.'

Browne thought enough time had been wasted. 'How old are you, Stocks?'

'Twelve, sir.'

'And you, Freebourne?'

'Fourteen.' He fingered his bruised but now bloodless nose.

Browne turned to Bellamy. 'Take this youth home and tell his mother not to let us catch him on these premises again until he's officially summoned back to school. You, Freebourne,' he added, turning round, 'can sit out in the corridor, under Constable Dean's eye until that projection on your face looks a bit more like a nose.'

The boy obeyed sulkily and his mother departed to express her indignation to her long-suffering colleagues. Browne heaved a huge sigh. 'One more to go. Let's beard this final lioness in her own den, too, shall we?'

Hunter held the door open and they walked round the corner to the domestic science room, where, within two minutes of their arrival, Meg Rivers presented herself. She came in confidently, took the seat at her own desk and invited the two policemen to draw up chairs of their own.

She sat composedly, looking forthright, attractive and eminently capable. The attraction lay, Browne decided, partly in the beautifully cut garments which she wore with such aplomb and partly in her superb self-command. She could have looked heavy and sallow but managed instead to give an impression of strength and energy. A clever hairdresser had introduced just sufficient light streaking to give a cheerful, dappled effect to hair that remained predominantly the dark brown that suited her. Browne remembered Virginia's judgment: 'Mrs Rivers has style and she will have when she's eighty.'

She had made her impression on the room in which she taught. Sinks and tiles gleamed, alternate gas and electric cookers lined one wall, all immaculate, a rail on each double desk held snowy tea-cloths and the walls displayed a colourful range of informative posters. A gaudy title, 'Hot Is Clean', seemed from the illustration below to refer to washing-up water although the rest of the print was too small for Browne to read from where he was sitting. An invitation to 'Brush up your technique' dealt, disappointingly Browne thought, with dental health. A predominantly blue sheet to his right advised Browne on 'Four ways to Healthy Eating' – less sugar, less salt, less fat, more fibre. Mrs Rivers followed his gaze and Browne remarked that, in his own schooldays, a good juicy steak had been judged to constitute the ideal meal.

She smiled. 'We think we know better, now, and, doubtless, in ten years' time, the new experts will be tutting over the damage done by fibre.'

Turning to the business in hand, Browne learned, from crisp questions and equally crisp replies, that Mrs Rivers had enjoyed a lively argument with her headmistress the previous evening about what should be done to enliven the shabby appearance of the old foyer. She had arrived at school at approximately eight forty, unlocked her equipment for the day and carried it to her room, then joined her colleagues in the staff room. She had done a quick check of her sixth-form tutor group at registration, then returned to her teaching room to prepare for a demonstration of microwave cooking for her first class.

Looking round, Browne saw no signs of an abandoned cookery demonstration, and, rightly interpreting his quizzical glance, Mrs Rivers gave a slightly rueful grin. 'I didn't realise the summons to the hall was about something quite so serious. We've been called together before for a Head's lecture when someone has behaved particularly badly. I thought it could well wait for five minutes or so and made the girls clear up and put everything away. They didn't take long over it; they're used to me.'

Browne nodded. 'That seems to cover the facts for the moment. Would you have said anyone in school had any reason to kill Miss Bland?'

'Well, no reason would justify murder. One or two had reason to wish her out of the way.'

'For example?'

'Why are you asking me? I'm a suspect.'

'True, but you seem a remarkably sensible and observant one, though that doesn't exonerate you.'

She absorbed this. 'There's Penny Stafford for a start. She's in a bit less trouble now, at least as far as yesterday's incident is concerned. And Geoff might let Kevin go on his course now. His own job will probably be easier, too, with a new head, unless he's unwise enough to apply for the post himself.' Aware that she was being led into indiscretion, she fell silent.

'Finally, Mrs Rivers, we've found some entries in Miss Bland's diary to meetings with someone whose initial is B. Have you any idea who it might refer to?'

Her prospective speculations were interrupted by a crash as a sudden movement dislodged her handbag from the chair arm where she had hooked it. For the third time that day, the contents of a handbag were spread before Browne. It was another black leather one and looked expensive, the kind the shops called an organiser bag with little separate pockets all with individual fastenings. Only the contents of the main middle section had spilled, and he gathered them up and handed them to her, a silver pen and two cheap ballpoints, handbag-size containers of a few expensive cosmetics, a leather diary and purse, a phial of low-calorie sweeteners and an envelope addressed to her, Mrs P.B.M. Rivers. Browne glanced at it and recalled his own pique as a youth at being denied an impressive array of initials and having only one given name. He had taken the sweeteners at first glance to be yet another supply of tranquillisers, but realised quickly that such things would not be the resort of the woman in front of him. She thanked him for retrieving her property, deftly stowed it away and returned, briefly, to his question. 'You can see from the list which staff have that initial. If it's not someone from school, then I have no idea. I know very little about her private life and I've certainly never been introduced to any of her friends.'

Browne thanked her and sent her back to the staff room. As she departed, Bellamy's head appeared round the door with the welcome news that Mrs Barstow's promised refreshments had arrived in the office. Returning there, they discovered not only a large pot of tea, but a plateful of beef sandwiches and an apple turnover of ample proportions. According to Bellamy, all their colleagues had been similarly provided for and suitable thanks offered. The bread was fresh and thickly buttered, the beef pink and moist and the pastry light. Browne made short work of his share as he outlined his plans for the evening.

'It's time we parted company. The interfering mother for me and for you a prowl round the exclusive new estate at Shepley Shay and in particular round the desirable residence just lately the property of Miss Bland. Bellamy and Jennie Smith have had a preliminary look round. Their report's on the table there. You'd better skim through it but I want you to give the place the once-over, then put someone onto the neighbours for information in general and on gentlemen visitors in particular.'

Not displeased with his lot, Hunter pushed his refilled mug across to Browne. 'Have you worked out the odds on this little collection of academics?'

Browne accepted the mug and considered. 'We've had a look at all the ones with the opportunity – although some had more than others. Maynard would have had to be fairly nifty to fit it in. White claims he only returned from the soccer pitch by the admin corridor, and that was after Miss Stafford had visited the study and the deed was done. Certainly, in all the comings and goings, no one saw him before that. Mrs Weston had the best opportunity but there's no discernible motive so far, and the same goes for Mrs Rivers.'

His meal finished, Hunter was walking about again. 'Miss Stafford is the only one with anything substantial to gain,' he contributed. 'The head seemed to be the only one who considered yesterday's little contretemps to be serious enough for drastic steps to be taken. I don't think she'd have the guts for bloody murder though.'

'They find the guts when they're desperate. And she had enough to take the letter.'

'That's true and she was very upset afterwards.'

Browne said slowly, feeling for the words to express his rather nebulous idea, 'The "persecuted" people like Miss Stafford usually feel, under all the melodrama and self-pity, a sort of elation at having pulled off something like this and got their own back. I haven't seen any sign of it in her. Not that I'd give any weight to such speculations.'

'Naturally not. What about Frayn? He's given us enough rope to hang him with.'

Browne grinned. 'It's probably his idea of fun. It seems rather an unsubtle killing for someone so sophisticated. I'd expect a more oblique approach, something neater, cleverer, less messy. And he does seem to have had some sympathy with her and influence over her. He probably had a fair bit of his own way under her régime.' Browne cast longing eyes over Hunter's abandoned piece of apple turnover.

Hunter ignored him. 'And Mrs Freebourne?'

'She wasn't on her own for long enough.'

'What about her and her mother together?'

Browne drained the teapot into his own mug. 'I doubt

it. I think her antipathy for her mother is genuine, and when her yokel offspring shambled in with his shirt front splattered with drippings from his unbeautiful nose her face bleached and froze. I'm sure she thought for a minute that he was the guilty party.'

Hunter relented, walked over to the desk and pushed his plate towards Browne. 'Would you like to finish the turnover, sir? It wouldn't do to offend Mrs Barstow.'

Browne turned his car left out of the school gates and negotiated the narrow strait in Moorside Rise where the dust-cart had held up his suspects earlier in the day. The evening was just beginning to draw in and the curious, yellowish light lent an exotic quality to the silhouettes even of the council houses at the bottom of the hill. Deprived of homework, the teenage population roamed around him and he decided that there was little point in the school remaining closed any longer. Maynard had requested a staff meeting for the next morning which he intended either Hunter or himself to attend. After that things could run normally again. He stifled a hope that Virginia would develop flu symptoms in the meantime. He turned left again at the bottom of the hill and parked neatly in front of a house in the middle of a terraced row.

The neatly painted gate clicked as he opened it and the curtain at the unlighted front window twitched and fell back into prim folds. On the pavement behind him, it was autumn; his feet had rustled and crackled through drifts of the season's debris. In the tiny plot in front of the house next door waves of yellow and purple bloom lapped against the top of a restraining wall. In the Corbys' garden he found himself in limbo. He wondered whether Mrs Corby rushed out to sweep up every leaf as it fell or whether she had disciplined the trees to drop no litter on her property. The pollarded lime just inside the gate was still green. It looked like a tree in a child's drawing, its sturdy trunk topped by an out-of-proportion, small ball of foliage. The Corbys were merciless gardeners. The lawn had not so much been trimmed as given a convict cut. Browne elaborated this fancy, walking up the narrow concrete path that suggested to him a neat centre parting in a short back and sides. There were not only no weeds but no plants in the borders, though under the window a bush of a species he failed to identify carried bulging buds which it endeavoured to restrain from bursting into unmannerly bloom. Browne compared it with his own garden, where unassuming clumps of Michaelmas daisies, shaggy outdoor chrysanthemums and dahlias cheerfully assisted the year in its transition from high summer to early winter.

Finding no knocker and no bell, Browne hammered on the gleaming paint of the door. Knowing he had been observed at the gate, he expected a speedy reaction, but he seemed to have been assigned to the category of caller whom Mrs Corby attended to in her own good time. As he waited, a spherical cat purred at his feet and Browne's attitude to the Corbys softened slightly as he bent to stroke it. When he stood up again, the door opened. With surprising skill the animal avoided the kick aimed at it and disappeared into a mass of late white saxifrage that cascaded over its owner's rockery.

'Don't you go encouraging that dirty creature. It spends half its life trying to get into my house. It can make its mess where it belongs. What do you want?' A scrawny figure stood in the doorway, of middle height, though she had probably been taller before age hunched her shoulders and bent her back. She had colourless remnants of hair, no longer brown and not having the substance to show up grey, arranged in a defiant but pathetic frizz, through which the scalp showed an indignant pink. The face it framed had its lines reinforced by the scowl it wore.

Browne, feeling a wave of aggression to match hers, showed her his card and curtly requested admission. Her avidity to hear about the latest developments at the school battled with her instinct to keep him on the doorstep, then she stepped back to let him in. The hall was so narrow that he had to draw himself in to avoid brushing against its pristine walls. Expecting the old woman's hospitality to be grudging, he was surprised to be shown into a tiny parlour, as hospital-clean as the hall and invited to make himself comfortable. She hurriedly covered a rubbed patch on the moquette chair arm with a cushion and tucked under her arm the one newspaper and piece of dark grey knitting that were lying on the matching sofa.

'I'm sorry we're in such a mess. We weren't expecting visitors.'

Browne forebore to argue with her and gratefully accepted the tea she offered. Whilst she busied herself in the kitchen, he carefully removed a damp leaf that was stuck to his shoe before it could mark the much vacuumed carpet. Looking for somewhere to dispose of it, he spied a decorative wicker wastebin under a gleaming coffee table. Inside it was a more functional container lined with a plastic bag and inside this the items of refuse were all wrapped in smaller bags. Unable to bring himself to sully this triumph of hygiene with his muddy leaf, Browne put it in his pocket.

As he bit back a pitying smile, the door opened to admit, he presumed, Mr Corby. He had probably been despatched at Browne's knock to put on a tie and he finished adjusting it as he sat down. Browne introduced himself as his wife brought in the tea. She poured it into china cups, highly decorated and obviously seconds, for the apple green and gilt borders on the saucers varied in width and depth of colour. The teaspoon, however, was of beautiful, heavy silver and Mrs Corby favoured him with a tight smile as he held it up and admired it.

'That's the rat-tail design.' She turned over her own spoon to indicate the way the handle tapered and came to a point over the back of the bowl of the spoon. 'I used to work at the firm in Sheffield where it was made. Not a dirty job, of course.'

Her husband grinned and spoke for the first time. 'Mine were, though.'

He was not encouraged to continue. 'The Constable doesn't want to hear about our past history.'

Browne bridled, then realised that, to her, any three-syllabled mode of address denoted high rank. She drank from her cup with her little finger sticking out and the glare she directed at her husband dared him, at his peril, to reveal any more of their humbler origins.

Browne drained his cup and smiled at her. 'If I had time, it would be very interesting. My own father worked in the Sheffield steel industry, but I really came to see if you could tell me any more than I know about the events at the school this morning.' He saw in her face an odd mixture of fear, curiosity and satisfaction. 'I understand you were up there at the relevant time.'

'Are you suggesting . . . ?'

'I'm suggesting that you may have some very important information to give me.'

This was obviously the right line to take. She readily admitted she had visited the biology lab just after ten to nine and found her daughter putting on protective clothing before attending to the bees. Mrs Weston had waved to her as she had passed the office window and she had nodded in acknowledgment. She was more reticent about the reason for her visit and Browne regretted pressing her when she became as voluble on the subject of her bad relations with her daughter as the latter had been.

'We let her go and get a first-class honours degree.' She paused to allow Browne time to be impressed both at their daughter's achievement and their own generosity. 'And now look at her.' She refilled Browne's cup self-righteously. 'Everyone said we should send her out to work and get something back for all we've done for her but we wanted to give her every advantage so that she could get a good job and everything nice.'

'You must be very proud of her now.'

'I might be if she hadn't got married. Not that there's anything wrong with being married to the right chap.' She gave her husband a proprietorial pat on the hand, and, having thrown him his crumb of comfort, waited for his grateful smile.

121

'Is your daughter unhappy, then?'

The mother clucked impatiently. 'Stands to reason, doesn't it? A houseful of children, all running riot and she has to leave them and go out to work. Of course, he has a job, for what it's worth – social worker!' Her tone classed it with the lower forms of prostitution. 'Getting paid peanuts for interfering with what doesn't concern him, whilst his own tribe are out till all hours, getting themselves into trouble because there's no one at home to teach them better.'

From what he had seen of the offspring, Browne considered that she might have a point. 'Wasn't it because you were concerned about one of them that you went to see your daughter?'

'I might as well have saved my breath. She won't hear any wrong of them. I came away more worried than I went. She told me young Neville was in trouble with Her Majesty across the corridor and she'd been threatening Glenys that he was going the right way to get expelled.'

'Oh, come on, Gertie.' They were both surprised by Mr Corby's intervention. 'They're not bad kids, and anyway, the Inspector hasn't come to talk about Glenys's children.' Browne's credentials lay beside the sugar basin and he had read them more carefully than his wife.

Browne elicited the information that Mrs Freebourne had seen her mother off the premises some time after five past nine. She had heard the duplicating machine. 'A real racket it was making!' She had seen no one until she had looked back from the school gate and seen 'our Glenys, talking to the young history teacher in the car park. Hadn't time to talk to me, her class was on its way, but plenty of time to spare for her fancy friends.'

'Perhaps they were discussing school business.' Browne rose to leave and thanked them for their help and refreshments. He obtained a juvenile pleasure from allowing the globular cat, hovering again at the door, to slip between his legs and escape down the hall into the Corbys' kitchen.

* * *

122

Sergeant Hunter left the school half an hour after the Inspector, having been left to arrange with Maynard the time of the next day's staff meeting and to hear what Mitchell had to say about his eavesdropping in the staff room. As he followed the route out of town to the village three miles away where Miss Bland had lived, Hunter reviewed the report of the upstart, Mitchell, and a tight knot of anger in his midriff made him uncharacteristically blind to the mysterious beauty through which he drove. Chimney-pots, trees, concrete lamp-stands and telegraph poles framed, with their elaborate tracery, a sky where the fading but luminous daylight did battle with the glow of burning sodium, each making the other seem irrelevant and the combination giving a feeling of unreality. Usually, Hunter was sensitive to such impressions, but now, those sections of his mind not employed with the management of accelerator, brake and clutch were busy with his grudge against the bumptious Mitchell. To think of him, achieving inspectorate level in five years! How would he function without the years of patient experience that should have taught him about human nature, good and bad? Hunter wondered what the school staff would think of Mitchell's rapid progress through the ranks. He had failed to impress many of them and they would have been less impressed still to hear his tittle-tattle about them. They hadn't given him much joy, concentrating only on matters of immediate importance, timetable adjustments, the transferring of Maynard's routine duties to his colleagues whilst he took over the responsibilities of headship. Some matters currently being dealt with were being carried through. The letters of complaint to various parents were to be signed and sent out. Mitchell had actually boasted about his parents receiving several such communications. School references were due to various universities on behalf of several sixth-formers, 'old Frayn's blue-eyed boys and girls'. Trust Mitchell to mock people who had succeeded in a field where he had failed.

Then Hunter smiled, in spite of himself, at the scene Mitchell had described of Mrs Rivers bustling about, getting the staff room into the same immaculate condition as her own domestic science room, and the caretaker's dreadful wife taking bristling offence at the implied accusation of her husband's negligence. 'Bustling' was the wrong word for Mrs Rivers, Hunter decided. She would have worked with economy of movement and speedy results.

Browne seemed to have taken a fancy to the coarse Mrs Barstow. He was often highly entertained by noisy, vulgar people who offended his own sensibilities. He supposed that was why he was so keen on Mitchell. Vitality, he said they had. Hunter sniffed. He had a different name for it.

The great respect he had for the Inspector and his own fair-mindedness, coming belatedly into play, made him admit that Mitchell did have some admirable qualities, but the admission fired rather than soothed his resentment. Did Browne not think well of himself? Where had he, Hunter, fallen short? He remembered the times when his superior officer had asked for and taken account of his opinion, had made use of his phenomenal memory. Now it looked as if the insufferable Mitchell would soon be making their partnership a threesome.

The part of his mind that was driving registered that he was passing from a forty m.p.h. to a thirty m.p.h. speed limit as he approached Shepley Shay. He made a conscious effort to relax and raised his right foot, watching the needle on the speedometer drop through fifty and forty down to the required speed. If he didn't want to be disciplined and demoted and have the despised Mitchell actually replacing him, he'd better concentrate on the job in hand.

Following Maynard's directions, he found the house without difficulty. The amber light from the streetlamps had gained precedence over the daylight, robbing the garden of colour, but sufficiently illuminating its neat lawns and flower-beds. After a pause to survey the general style of the building he used the keys from Miss Bland's handbag to let himself in and made a preliminary inspection of the ground floor. The whole property struck him as the joint production of a clever architect, a skilful builder, a competent landscape gardener and a smart interior designer. Everything was in the best of taste, chosen because it fitted in with the general scheme of genteel comfort. The only idiosyncrasy was the forest of greenery which began in the hall and continued into the living-room which ran the length of the house. The plants all flourished but for one, standing on a table at the dining end of the room, magnificent but unhappy. He considered the furnishings and ornaments in the room conventional until he came to the picture of the poppies. His eyes were drawn to it and he knew it was remarkable without knowing why. His interests lay more with literature and music than with painting but he was sufficiently sensitive and intelligent not to undervalue what he couldn't understand. After a few seconds' rapt concentration, he pulled his mind back to his job and began a systematic examination.

He noticed that a wall-chart calendar, pinned to the back of the door, had Miss Bland's appointments with B entered on it. It occurred to him that the reason for this double recording was not so much to avoid forgetting the engagements as an immature wish to exult in them. But why write only his initial? And why could no one who had yet been asked shed any light on his identity? He had an idea that such an unforthcoming, reserved person, as Miss Bland seemed so far to have been, might have poured out her hopes, secrets, grievances, in a jumbo-sized diary. He sought such a volume, hopefully, in the drawers of the sideboard at the dining end and the bookcases at the opposite end of the living-room but with no success. He found only a good stock of table linen, heavy steel cutlery, glasses for all manner of occasions and an extremely well-stocked drinks cupboard.

He moved to the kitchen and found himself surrounded by matching cream units with imitation marble tops. The double sink unit was spotless, its cream plastic surface dry. The dishwasher contained breakfast dishes, neatly racked. The walls, tiled in cream and lemon, and the speckled fawn floor were rescued from insipidity by the decorator's clever use of apple green on the ceiling. Perhaps the plants, which echoed the greenness and drew attention to it, had been Miss Bland's idea, or, more likely, Hunter thought, she had created the effect without being aware of it. There were drawers full of drying-cloths adorned with pictures and cartoons and cupboards filled with tins and raw materials sufficient to withstand a siege. The refrigerator and deep-freeze were equally well stocked.

Hunter smiled, remembering the plump figure, at a plastic apron hanging on the door bearing the emblem 'A Diet is Too Little of a Good Thing'. At her age, such a garment struck him as childish and pathetic. There was evidence that she had enjoyed cooking. The collection of herbs, spices and gadgets outdid his wife's in amount and variety.

His search and his speculations were interrupted by a complicated chime of bells. He grimaced at the vulgarity. Here was something not chosen by the acme of discrimination responsible for the rest of the house. He opened the door and was confronted by a fair young man who half bowed and gesticulated with both arms before he spoke, so that the French accent came as little surprise.

'So, you are the gentleman friend of Miss Bland?'

'I might be. What can I do for you?'

'You could please give me the papers of this morning, if she has finished them. She gives them to me. I read all the English newspapers.'

'Good for you, but she isn't here at the moment and I think she has left the morning paper at school.'

He stood, looking crestfallen, as though this breakdown in his system rendered any further newspaper-reading point-less. His T-shirt, emblazoned with an invitation to try a particular brand of French beer, looked hardly warm enough for an autumn evening in Yorkshire but there were no goose-pimples on his muscular arms. He blinked through his thick, rimless lenses and fidgeted and Hunter, surmising that jeans so indecently tight must have been put on as either a penance or a dare, stood back and opened the door wider.

'Come in for a few minutes. I'm Detective Sergeant Hunter.'

'And I am Denis Lacoste, but in England I answer only to Deniss.' He stressed the English pronunciation and winked at Hunter. 'So, she has fallen out with her other lover and taken a policeman?'

Misinterpreting the 'What other lover?' which Hunter failed to bite back, Monsieur Lacoste winked again and shrugged. 'I have let the cat out of the bag? It is useless to go back on it.'

'It is, indeed. I'll make a cup of coffee, and you, my friend, had better tell me about the other lover.'

Seemingly oblivious of the strain on his seams and the physical pain it must have caused him, Lacoste lowered his buttocks on to a kitchen stool and awaited Hunter's catechism. Hunter filled the kettle and took out a jar of instant coffee.

'How long has she been seeing him? What's his name? Where does he live?'

The Frenchman blinked again and thought. 'I see him only in the dark when he brings her home. She thinks I do not know about it and so I let her think. His name I do not know, not where he lives. They arrive always in her car and he departs always in a taxi.'

'What does he look like?'

This time, the hesitation was longer. 'I would not wish you to go and fight with him, nor to make her angry because I tell you. I think perhaps I leave the coffee and go now.'

Hunter poured boiling water into the cups and indicated that Lacoste should remain seated. 'I'm afraid I have to give you some bad news. Miss Bland is dead. She died in school this morning.'

It was impossible to read the expression in the Frenchman's eyes through the thick, distorting lenses. 'She was ill, then? She met with an accident?'

'She met with an attacker who hit her over the head with a model cat.'

Lacoste's reaction to this bald fact was disapproval rather than horror. 'It is so violent, her school?'

'Someone who was in it this morning certainly is.'

'And the little cat. Was it the one she showed me from the museum at London?' Now he seemed merely curious.

Hunter pushed a mug of coffee across the table. 'Very likely it was. Tell me what you know about it.'

He checked on his new position before answering. 'So you, a policeman, are here to investigate a killing?'

Hunter nodded. 'That's right. And the cat?'

'I think it was a gift of the lover. In the summer holiday she visited at London and she showed it to me when I came for the newspaper. It made her smile to look at it.'

'Did she tell you that it was a present?'

'Yes, but she did not say from the lover. She was thinking that I had not seen him, but after the London visiting I see him sometimes.'

'How well did you know her yourself?'

'Not well. I meet her one Sunday in the church and she was offering to tell me the best newspapers and magazines to look at and then, I was collecting them after school.'

Hunter produced his credentials which were examined with lively interest, and managed to extract a fairly detailed description of Miss Bland's male visitor in exchange for some information about English police procedure before Lacoste took his leave. He resumed his search, taking the bathroom next.

It was minute and contained a scaled-down bath with a shower. The cream wall tiles, bathside and shower curtain were sprigged with pink rosebuds and green leaves. Over a heated double towel rail, matching green and pink towels hung. This room contained only one plant, a lush fern, perched on the corner of the bath, its leaves falling down into it. The bathroom was the child of its designer, a minor work of art, a confection. To it, its owner had added just one object, a blue and white striped washbag from which protruded a tube of toothpaste and a large bottle of anti-dandruff shampoo. A tiny wall cabinet contained deodorant, bath cleaner and aspirins and there was nowhere that anything could be concealed.

Hunter proceeded to the bedroom. Its built-in furniture

was light-coloured, sandalwood, Hunter guessed, which contrasted pleasantly with the deep coral wall areas, the largest of which was broken by a flower print on a white mount. No possessions were scattered about; the room was painfully tidy. Hunter set to work on the drawers. Starting at the top he turned up extensive stocks of underwear, mostly from Marks and Spencers, all of it serviceable and substantial. Below were prim Viyella blouses and heavy sweaters. No winter's chill would have crept up unexpectedly on this lady. The dressing-table top was bare but in the drawer were a tin of talcum powder and a jar of cold cream. A plastic pouch with a zip held a replacement block of the powder cream found in Miss Bland's handbag and two chaste pink lipsticks but no eye make-up.

A full-length towelling dressing-gown hung behind the door.

The bedside cabinet, with its cupboard and two small drawers, Hunter saved till last. Here, if anywhere, he would find the letters, diary, photographs he so hoped to show to Browne. In the cupboard was an old chocolate box, complete with coy kitten and full of embroidered handkerchiefs. Beside it was a bottle of Mogadon. Hunter noted that it had been issued by the same local chemist as had supplied the tranquillisers in the handbag. The top drawer did disclose two photographs, close-ups of a small boy with features not unlike Miss Bland's. They were more handsome in the male version.

Before opening the bottom drawer, Hunter, like a small boy himself, closed his eyes and wished. What he found was a surprise but not a disappointment. The satin pants and bra were a vivid sea green, beautifully embroidered, brief, provocative and expensive. The nightdress and négligé, carefully folded, were of cerise silk. He took them out and imagined Miss Bland encased in them. The idea was neither pathetic nor amusing. 'Butch' had been Mitchell's description of Miss Bland's type, accurate as slang so often is. She was unattractive because she was self-conscious and unhappy and had never learned to make the best of herself.

These garments had been chosen by someone who knew what would flatter her and could afford to pay for it. The singing colours would have dramatised the dark complexion and made her glow. Hunter recognised that he had run up against someone with flair and imagination.

The garments were obviously freshly laundered and unlikely to retain any evidence by which the lab could trace them to their donor. Nevertheless, he sealed each of them carefully in a plastic bag, satisfied that the gods had granted his wish.

Chapter 8

Detective Constable Mitchell was almost ready to keep his date with his current girlfriend. Although her charms were begining to pall, he had no less enthusiasm for the preparation of his person for public view. He inspected his black jeans for marks, pulled his clean white sweater straight and smooth over his flat stomach and checked that the collar of his black shirt was arranged sufficiently casually. He was not satisfied with the unruly behaviour of his freshly washed hair. It always stuck out when it was clean.

He tapped on his sister's bedroom door to make sure she was downstairs, crept over to her dressing-table and selected the hairspray from an assortment of pressurised cans. Holding down his hair with his left hand, he squirted with his right until his locks gave up the struggle against gravity and Freon and lay flat. Wrinkling his nose at the heavy, flowery perfume he crept back to his own room from which he made a noisy exit. He called goodbye to the family gathered in front of the television set and left the house.

What little keenness he had had for his outing was fast evaporating; he would far rather have stayed in. He felt there was more than an even chance that the chief might want to chat to him about the Bland case. He knew better than anyone working on it the geography of the school, the personalities of the people employed there, their way of doing things, their relationships with each other and the normal routine of a typical day. He had had it drilled into him that to discover the perpetrator of a crime, you had to look for someone who had deviated from what was usual.

He hadn't come up with anything yet, though. Perhaps it was as well not to be available for old Browne's questions until he had something ready to suggest. Besides, there was no way he dared stand Mel up. They hadn't exactly behaved with discretion and if she decided to get her own back by telling all, he could forget all about accelerated promotion.

He tried to remember why she had attracted him in the first place. He supposed they'd both been rebels. He'd admired the spirit it required in the daughter of a teacher to display the brassy bleached hair, the provocative necklines and the insolent manner that marked her out. He was tired of rebellion now, though. He wanted to settle down and do well in his job. Even at school, he'd been getting tired of the way everyone looked to him to supply the amusing disruptions when, sometimes, he'd been quite keen to settle to his work. He supposed it was his own fault that most of the staff hadn't liked him and, on the whole, he had deserved the punishments he was constantly given. Some staff, though, had been quite entertained by his chirpy insolence. Maynard had given him some breaks and some good advice and Frayn hadn't been a bad old stick. At least his lessons were never boring. No one ever caused bother in his classes. If you did you missed the laughs, or, worse still, had them directed against you. He couldn't see either Frayn or Maynard as killers. Frayn punished with his tongue, not his fists and Maynard wouldn't be unchivalrous to a woman in any way, never mind kill her. He'd really like the killer to be Mrs Weston, although that wasn't likely. Another head would put her back in her place. She'd become a power in the land under this set-up. Most kids were more scared of getting on the wrong side of her than of being in trouble with the Head, and that went for half the staff, too. He couldn't understand her rudeness to Maynard or why he took it from her. If Maynard killed anyone it should be Weston.

Mitchell grinned as he thought how dismayed the staff would be if they realised how closely observed and well understood they were by their senior pupils. What motives for murder might the others have? Maybe Mrs Freebourne did it because that awful brother of Mel's had been pinching again and Miss Bland was threatening to bring in the police. She was a biologist. She'd know where to hit someone to lay them out at one blow. She might work out, too, that crushed blood vessels don't spurt blood straight away if you only hit each spot once. It couldn't be feeble old Stafford, and Mrs Rivers would have stayed to clean up the desk and leave everything just so.

He smiled at this fancy and moved on to consider Mr White. He was a character who knew what he wanted and went straight out to get it. Look at the way the soccer and athletics teams had shot up the ladder in the league competitions since he'd been in charge of things. But Miss Bland had been pleased with his success and hadn't interfered with his plans as far as Mitchell could see. He wished he could produce someone with motive and opportunity that the Inspector hadn't considered. What about Bouncing Barstow? Unfortunately, she hadn't bounced along at the relevant time, or, if she had, she'd been unusually quiet about it.

Mitchell turned a corner and now he could see Melanie waiting for him, a cigarette dangling from her fingers, eyeing up and down the passing boys who called out and whistled at the amount of leg she displayed. Three months ago, he'd been proud to possess a girl so obviously admired. Now he wished with all his might that she'd go off with one of the whistlers and give him an excuse for ending it. Why didn't he do it anyway? He was tempted but she'd fight like an alley cat.

A daring thought occurred to him. When he'd found a way to deal with Mel, why not have a whirl with Ginny Browne? Now, there was a firecracker. She didn't have to resort to bleached hair and practically non-existent skirts. She could afford to be choosy, though. He'd have to give some thought to how to interest her. There was no hurry. To start now would cause too many unwanted complications in this case. He'd wait till it was solved and in the meantime

133

he'd better see if he could provoke Mel sufficiently for her to take the initiative and finish with him herself.

By the time Hunter was ready to leave Miss Bland's house, the sodium lamps had won their battle with the fading daylight and were ruling their night-time kingdom. They were reflected by the beginnings of a frost and Hunter pulled his coat collar closer round his neck. There was a mid-evening lull in the main road traffic and in fifteen minutes' time he was parking outside the station in the hope of displaying to Browne the contents of his plastic bags. He was disappointed to learn that Browne had been and gone, having, according to Tuckey, the station Sergeant, spent most of his short visit in his office on the telephone. He left a message, in case Browne returned, that he would ring him later from home, then set off there, hoping that Annette would have allowed Fliss to stay up a little beyond her usual bedtime.

Annette looked relieved to see him and, in spite of the fact that he was tired and hungry, glanced up in the direction of their daughter's bedroom. 'She's in bed but she's a bit upset about some quarrel at school. She thinks you're going to wave a magic wand and make everything right again.'

He smiled and took the stairs two at a time, his energy renewed by his being on home ground again. 'There you are, you see,' he greeted his daughter. 'I usually manage to arrive just before you have to go to sleep.'

Two mournful eyes regarded him out of a tear-streaked face. 'Something happened today, something nasty.'

He perched on the edge of the bed. 'Tell me about it.'

She drew a quivering sigh. 'Miss Monks took my writing book and showed it to everyone in the class. She said, "If everyone's work was as neat and careful as Felicity Hunter's, I would have a lot less work to do." '

As his daughter, soft lisp and tired droop abandoned, produced a creditable imitation of Miss Monks's strident tones and hectoring manner, Hunter bit his lip. 'But that isn't nasty. What is there to cry about?'

The tears flowed afresh. 'Because nobody in the class will talk to me now. They say I'm teacher's pet.' She buried her sobs in the pillow.

Hunter tilted her face towards him and wiped her eyes. 'They're only jealous. You must be proud of having the best book in the class, but it would be as well not to say so. Perhaps you could say something nice about someone else's work tomorrow.'

Fliss considered this remedy, then rejected it in favour of her own. 'No. I shall put a lot of blots on mine tomorrow and then Sally and I will be friends again.' This suggestion seemed to please her. She pulled the sheet up under her chin. 'Good night, Daddy.' She was asleep when he closed the bedroom door.

The family meal was over and, as he came downstairs, he could hear Annette in the kitchen, preparing a tray for him. At the dining-room table sat eleven-year-old Tim, crowned with a large, peaked motoring cap which he must have purloined from the car again. Hunter wondered, not for the first time, from whom his son had inherited the ears which stuck out and prevented the cap from sinking low enough to obscure his vision. Hunter's own ears were neat and flat and so were Annette's.

He tweaked the hair growing over the boy's collar but provoked no response. Tim sat, lips moving, eyes closed, as though in a trance. Hunter could just make out the chanted words.

> Season of mists and mellow fruitfulness,
> Close bosom friend of the maturing sun
> Conspiring with him how to load and bless . . .

The boy's right fist beat the table on the strong beat of each iambic foot. When the performance stopped because of Tim's need to refresh his memory with a glance at his book, Hunter approached him again.

'Whose homework are you doing?'

'Old Frayn's.'

'Do you understand what it's about?'

Tim seemed to find the question pointless. 'He didn't tell us to understand it. He told us to learn it.'

As Hunter accepted his supper tray, he made a mental note to discuss with Frayn his ideas on the proper way to introduce children to the Romantic poets. As he bit into a wafer-thin slice of bread and butter, the telephone rang. Annette went out to answer it, not returning until he had refilled his cup and pushed the tray away.

'That was the big white chief. You're invited for beer and baring of souls at his place. Being a good police wife, I told him I didn't mind.'

When Browne left the Corbys he drove to the station and paid a visit to the incident room. Passing along to his office he had an interesting telephone conversation with the pathologist, then rang Hannah to announce his impending arrival. When, at last, he got home, he too found his dining-room table monopolised by homework. He opened his mouth to protest that his daughter had been provided with a room of her own which contained a perfectly adequate desk, but he bit back his rebuke at the sight of her rapt face. He always found it a moving experience to watch another person completely absorbed in his or her own mental activity. Virginia's complete unawareness of herself as she sought the right phrase to capture her idea gave her a special vulnerability and yet, at the same time, it rendered her completely unreachable and safe. Her right hand scribbled and her left played, involuntarily, with a lock of hair.

He surveyed her complacently. As always, she had made vigorous efforts to destroy an inborn aura of well-scrubbed wholesomeness. Tonight's attempt included patched and faded jeans and canvas shoes that were threadbare over each big toe. It annoyed her to have inherited his springy, curly dark hair, and she frequently had it all but shaved off. Fortunately, like his, it grew very quickly and her life was too full for her to be always at the hairdresser. He turned round to find his wife standing behind him and smiled up at her.

At five feet nine, Browne had not seen fit to restrict his choice of wife to the women of his acquaintance who were smaller than himself and was too self-assured to be put out because his wife topped him by an inch and his daughter promised to do so by more. Nor did Hannah creep around in flat-heeled shoes, head bowed. He had been devastated in his teens when he realised that he was unlikely to achieve the five feet ten demanded in recruits to his chosen profession. Then he had found his salvation in the Metropolitan Police, where the work was tough, not so many candidates offered themselves, and the requirements, so far as height was concerned, had not been so stringent. It had been a hard school for an eighteen-year-old but Browne had enjoyed his baptism by fire and was grateful for what he had learned. As his son, now away at university, had been fond of pointing out, if he had married a tiny girl, the consequent brood of pygmy sons would not have appreciated being the result of their father's vanity. Alex, either through Hannah's genes or his self-imposed physical training, had eventually achieved a respectable five feet eleven, but throughout his childhood, he had existed in fear of his sister, three years younger, outgrowing him.

Leaving their daughter to complete her work undisturbed they went back into the kitchen where Browne swiftly despatched cheese and pickles and home-made fruit-cake. Hannah did odd jobs at the work bench, diverting him with the highlights of her day and tacitly giving him the opportunity, which he ignored, of describing his own.

After a while, Virginia came in and took a can of lager from the fridge. She leaned against the door, pulling the ring and drinking from the can.

Browne made the mock-disapproving noises expected of him. 'I hope you don't drink that stuff in the Owl when you sneak in after school lunch.'

She grinned at him, displaying small, perfect teeth. 'Fat chance! I wear you like a badge. They think you send me round the pubs on spying missions. I always know when there's any under-age drinking going on – the rest of the sixth sneak off without me. They know they won't get served if I'm with them. I'd better get back to that Chaucer.'

'Just a minute.' He turned his chair round and faced her.

Virginia sighed, then addressed him with the tolerance and kindness of a lively adolescent who knew she hadn't done too badly in the parent stakes and must show due appreciation. 'I know what you're going to say. You say it every night. You change the order sometimes but you always complain about the same things.'

Browne was amused. 'You're wrong this time. I just want to know if you noticed anything in the school this morning, before Mr Maynard announced Miss Bland's death, that was at all out of step, not the usual thing.'

Virginia considered, then shook her head. 'I wish I'd noticed something significant that would solve the case for you. Then perhaps you'd realise you need me now instead of "There's plenty of time for the force when you've finished university." Anyway, I didn't. I dossed around in the common room, then went to registration. Mr Collins was waiting for us and marked us present. He made Chris take his earring out but that's the usual routine. Then he went with us down to assembly. Her Majesty didn't turn up and Maynie and Blythe Spirit had a summit conference on the platform. Then they got the hymn from Mr Chandler by semaphore and we had the deadly boring assembly you always have when someone's doing it on the spur of the moment and making it up as they go on. And some of them do go on. Maynie's not so bad. That's all.'

Browne let her go but a minute later she stuck her head round the door again. 'Val and Dave were on assembly duty. Try them.'

'Valerie Kelsey and David Draper?'

'That's right.'

As her head disappeared, Browne heard Hunter's car draw up outside and made for the cellar where he kept his supply of home brew.

He entertained his subordinate in the tiny room under the stairs which he had promised himself for a study even before

138

he had talked Hannah into agreeing to buy the house. It was over-full although it contained only a desk, a bookcase, two armchairs and a standard lamp. Having filled two glasses, Browne apologised for calling Hunter out again at the end of a long day.

Hunter, flattered by the invitation and full of his discovery, was not at all put out. 'It's much pleasanter here than at the station, sir. It doesn't feel so much like work.'

Both of them knew that for up to a week, evidence would accumulate and the background to the crime would be filled in. If the killer's name were not filled in too, then after eight or nine days the probability of discovering it receded. Browne half emptied his glass and placed it on the desk.

'I had a call from the lab whilst I was at the station. The PM's finished.'

'And?'

'It confirms all that Dr Ledgard surmised. And would you believe that that pillar of society, our offspring's revered headmistress, was not, of recent weeks, a virgin?'

Hunter was disappointed. His own discovery had lost its impact. Nevertheless, he produced his little packs of skimpy underwear with as much of a flourish as he could manage. 'Well, sir, if she had been, she wouldn't have remained one long in these.'

Browne examined them, showing a gratifying interest and listened to Hunter's account of his findings at Shepley Shay.

'So far, so good. We'll see what the lab can make of these sinful scraps. We're bound to come up with B before long. What sort of a description did your French friend produce?'

'With many ifs and buts and protestations that he'd only seen him in the dark, he managed to recollect grey hair, a tall broad build with wide shoulders and extremely well cut clothes.'

'Our friend is probably a snazzy dresser if he managed to impress a Frenchman,' Browne commented. 'Well, it's a start. It means she hasn't been playing Miss Stafford's game and we needn't seek her gentleman friend in the sixthform.' He refilled their glasses. 'Let's' take stock, then. This, of course, is the point where the fictional detective, through superhuman powers of deduction – or is the hunch back in literary fashion now to counteract the clinical approach of the real thing? – would whisper a name to his Sergeant who would then confine his activities to collecting enough evidence for a conviction. I do, I'm afraid, have a gut feeling about one thing, though I shan't allow it to prejudice the investigation. I don't think Freebourne is our customer.'

'She's left-handed,' Hunter put in.

'Thank you for that shred of justifying evidence. I also believe that our killer is definitely someone employed at the school. All the same, there's a house-to-house enquiry going on at the moment and continuing tomorrow to see if anyone who had no business there was seen going into the school or hanging around it. We'll have some men on the knocker at Shepley Shay too, tomorrow. We'll see what sort of picture of Miss Bland her neighbours can produce.'

Hunter nursed his empty glass awkwardly, loath to put it down in case the Inspector took it as a hint that his hospitality was wanting. Browne's mind was on other things.

'Now then, let's spend a few minutes working out who came along that corridor this morning and in what order.'

'It's as though someone choreographed it,' Hunter offered, 'with solo dancers on the stage in turn.'

Browne gaped at him, but Hunter, oblivious, had found another analogy that took his fancy. 'It's a bit like the screen scene in *School for Scandal*. I did it for A level. Most of the characters are hidden away and they pop out in turn.'

Browne was amused. 'You should have produced all this in front of Frayn when he was spouting Shakespeare at me. It would have kept our end up a bit. You're quite a lot like some of the story-book detectives he was sure I wouldn't be familiar with. You can quote fancy plays like Wexford, you're as tall as Rory Alleyn, as blond as Wimsey and you have all the fastidiousness of Dalgleish. You haven't written a slim volume of verse, have you?'

Hunter didn't answer, silenced by his astonishment that Browne not only knew about but shared his weakness for their fictional counterparts.

Browne recalled him to the task in hand. 'Let's make a timetable.'

Hunter knew how to interpret the Inspector's 'Let's' and obediently took out a notebook and pen for his dictation.

'Mrs Weston arrives first and goes to her office. Through the window, she sees the lab technician arrive and hears her go into the prep room across the corridor. What happened to her after that?'

'She's friendly with Mrs Barstow. Having checked that there was no apparatus to set up for the first two lessons she went to the kitchen for a chat and joined in the merry breakfast party. All safely checked and vouched for.'

Browne nodded. 'Next, Miss Bland appears, later than usual. Mrs Weston makes coffee and each of them drinks in her own room with the connecting door ajar. At eight fifty the registration bell goes, Mrs Freebourne comes up the corridor and into the biology lab. Then Mrs Corby turns up, observed through the window by Mrs Weston.'

Hunter's pen flew.

'Next, Frayn arrives in Mrs Weston's office, leaving his coat and an exam stencil for duplicating. Mrs Weston goes up the corridor the other way to the duplicating room, turns at the door and watches Frayn going through the fire doors, jacketless, on the way to pick up his gown. Shirt-sleeves on the corridor are not considered proper. Coming from the staff room to the admin corridor, Miss Stafford passes Frayn going the other way. She goes to the office to notify her intention of going home. Frayn continues, past the staff room, to assembly in the hall. Miss Stafford enters the office and finds Mrs Weston gone. She must have realised from the noise where she was, but she chooses to knock on Miss Bland's door and look round it. According to her, she sees the body, takes the Head's letter of resignation under the impression that it concerns herself and buzzes off.

'Mrs Freebourne has, at some point, gone out to see her mother off the premises and comes in to find Miss Stafford in extremis. She sees her to her car and promises to make her excuses to the Head. Presumably Miss Stafford didn't explain that this wouldn't be possible. Mrs Freebourne uses the internal phone in her prep room to summon the caretaker to clean up. As he arrives, White comes down the corridor from the opposite direction, taking a short cut to the staff room from the soccer pitch. Whilst still in the staff room he has seen Frayn, crossing the road on his way home.

'Assembly finishes and the children leave the hall. Mrs Weston returns to her office with the completed exam papers and sets to work on Frayn's coat. Staff, except those who are free, and children go to first lesson. Finally, Maynard arrives at the office and he and Mrs Weston discover the body. End of timetable. Your shorthand still up to all that?'

Hunter stopped scribbling and flexed his cramped hand as he nodded.

'Right. Several staff noticed and commented on the Head's late arrival, so I think we can accept Mrs Weston's assertion that she was alive at a quarter to nine. We know that she was dead by half past nine. If we believe Miss Stafford's second story, the time is narrowed much more. If she did it we know when. If she didn't, presumably she was telling the truth when she claimed to have seen the body just after nine. Otherwise she wouldn't have been so upset, in every sense, and she wouldn't have been able to remove the letter. Does that exonerate anybody?'

The two men concentrated. Browne sat motionless, staring at his hands. Hunter, prevented by his cramped circumstances from pacing, stood by the desk and drummed his fingers. He took over the reasoning aloud.

'Corby or Freebourne could have slipped across during the vital few minutes, but only if they were in league.'

'That doesn't seem likely,' Browne objected.

'Oh, I don't know. Maybe they're inventing their antagonism to confuse us.'

142

'With the rest of the staff in league with them?'

Hunter surrendered the point. 'Mrs Weston could have slipped back, leaving her machine to its own devices. Mrs Rivers could have come along from her room round the corner. Frayne could have returned after Mrs Weston had stopped watching him and Maynard was briefly on the bottom corridor near the fire doors "maintaining a staff presence" as he calls it and rounding up his conscientious objectors to morning worship. That leaves White, who says he was outside, but we only have his word that he didn't go out by the admin corridor as well as returning that way.'

Browne sat forward in his chair. 'No! Wait a minute. White left after Stafford and we know he stayed in the staff room until Frayn had left school. I think we can forget him if we accept that Miss Bland was dead by just after nine o'clock.'

They sat silent, checking again that they were justified in crossing off one suspect. Browne reflected that never before had his search for a murderer been so neatly concentrated nor the period of time that his suspects had to account for been so short. After some minutes he said, 'All right, we'll forget White. As far as the rest are concerned, opportunity being equal, we're back to motive, and, in particular, motive for killing her at that time. It was taking a great risk to do it at the beginning of a working day, when any one of a score of people might interrupt or notice. Why not wait until after school? Scrounge a lift from her? Visit her at home after dark? There must have been an imperative reason for despatching her at once, or else it was done in a rage or panic on the spur of the moment.'

He glared at Hunter who, chidden, stopped drumming his fingers and spoke instead. 'I can't think of a serious motive for him but Frayn was the person who created a situation that would mask the noise of an attack. He knew that he could charm any female, even Mrs Weston, into doing him a favour. He knew the machine would provide a clamour for at least five minutes.'

'So did Mrs Weston. Perhaps she'd been waiting for an opportunity and this was it.'

'But she had even less motive. The general opinion is that she was king of the castle here and any change in management was likely to cut her down to size.'

Browne shook his head. 'We haven't had time yet to ferret out half the possible motives. I can't think further than Frayn's going home at the vital time, stripping off and showering. Who the hell, when he's feeling randy, especially if he has a time-limit, quenches his ardour with a shower?'

Hunter made no reply and, looking up, Browne saw that he had coloured faintly. He waited, agog.

'Well, I do,' he offered after some seconds. 'Annette's fastidious. Besides, it's more . . . well, never mind.'

Remembering his meeting with Kate Frayn, it occurred to Browne that she might well be fastidious too. He took pity on the embarrassed Hunter and changed the subject. 'The trouble is, Frayn's one of the only two people we've questioned who seemed to have any fondness or respect for Miss Bland and he seemed genuinely upset when I encountered him in the staff room and told him what had happened, though he covered up with his usual patter. And it doesn't seem his sort of crime. I could see Freebourne doing such a thing in a panic, though I don't think she did on this occasion, or White in a temper, or Rivers because she'd decided it was deserved. But Frayn would plan something subtle and laugh to himself whilst we tried to decide whether we had a case of murder on our hands or just an unfortunate accident.'

Hunter nodded. 'So what now, then, sir?'

'Well you, my lad, will spend tomorrow morning sitting in on an interesting staff meeting, ostensibly to check that nothing they arrange will hold up our enquiry, but really to keep your eyes skinned and your ears open as they talk more informally and are, hopefully, a little less on their guard.'

'And you, sir?'

'I'm getting a bit bored with things in Cloughton. I think I'll have a day trip to London.'

144

Hunter did not rise to this. 'You're seeing her parents?'

'For my sins, I'm seeing her parents.'

On his way out, a twinkle in his eye, Hunter suddenly asked, 'Sir, what quality do I share with Poirot?'

Browne matched the twinkle. 'His cockiness, of course.'

Chapter 9

Bella Barstow, her duties at the school finished for the time being, let herself in at the back door that opened into her small and spotless kitchen. She had enjoyed her eventful day but now her varicose veins were beginning to spoil her performance as a woman in her prime. She removed her court shoes with their teetering heels, placed them neatly under the table and sank down on the sofa in front of the fire, arranging her legs along its length. Then she looked up at the armchair opposite and regarded the portions of her husband that stuck out round a double page spread of the *Sun*. His stockinged feet rested on a cushion, ham fists clutched the far edges of each page and a shiny dome fringed with grey appeared above, surrounded by a haze of smoke from an evil-smelling pipe which she knew would be gripped in his teeth.

'Well, like I always say,' she offered conversationally, 'there's never no time to get bored in a school full o' kids. I like a bit o' life, though it's a bit o' t'other thing that's livened things up today.'

Quite satisfied with Mr Barstow's grunted response, she leaned forward to switch on the television set, raising her voice to make it heard over the background music to a cops and robbers chase. 'I reckon the cops they sent up to t'school are a sight dishier than that lot.' She jerked a thumb to indicate a close-up shot of the policeman behind the wheel. 'They was well worth a few brews and the odd sandwich.' Mr Barstow encouraged his wife with a further grunt as she settled herself against a cushion.

'I'd advise 'em to leave well alone, though,' she went on. 'Mr Maynard'll manage things quite well now that Madam's out of the way. Someone's done us all a favour.'

'Just so long as they only want the place open during my usual hours. If they expect me to be chasing about after them half the night I'll be demanding some overtime from somebody.' He felt sufficiently strongly about this possible imposition on his good nature to release the pipe from his locked teeth, but his wife was unimpressed by the threat.

'Oh, aye? You'll do a lot wi' a big stick and a box of eggs. What do you think their 'ighnesses are doing now?'

'Seein' if any of them staff 'ave records, mebbe.'

'Not the cops, the teachers. I bet old Frayn's down at the pub, tellin' everybody 'ow quickly 'e'd solve it. And the Stafford woman'll be weepin' on somebody's shoulder.'

Mr Barstow prepared to return his pipe to its proper place. 'Ah, well, it's no business of our'n.' He retreated behind his paper again and Mrs Barstow, having stimulated him to speech, felt she had received her due from him and returned her attention to the screen.

She had speculated reasonably accurately on Penny Stafford's intentions. When Browne finally gave permission for the detained staff to go home, the young history mistress resentfully watched her colleagues disperse. No one was in the least concerned about the shock she'd suffered. She was beginning to feel quite ill again. It was too much to be left to drive home alone. She was sure she was going to be sick again. She went to the cloakroom door and leaned against it with her eyes closed, her anger mounting as the staff departed severally without seeming to notice her plight. She resented, most of all, Maynard's 'Goodnight, Penny. See you tomorrow.' He was deliberately ignoring the fact that she wasn't fit to be left alone. He was in charge now. It was his responsibility to make sure everyone got home safely. He was going to be no better to work for than Miss Bland.

Opening her eyes a crack, to see if any potential sympathisers remained, she found herself being regarded, cheerfully, by Bella Barstow. 'Night, Miss Stafford,' the impertinent woman bawled at her. 'You 'aven't left Mr Barstow no more cleaning up in there, 'ave you?' Fuelled by her fury, Miss Stafford walked out to her car and climbed in. She drove cautiously the mile to her flat and rang her sister to describe the symptoms of shock the events of the day had produced and the heartless way they'd been disregarded. Having failed to induce that long-suffering relative to abandon her young family and come on a mission of mercy, she made herself a cup of tea. She put it on a tray and, after a few seconds' hesitation, added a packet of chocolate biscuits and the rest of yesterday's cake. She had been wondering if she might have a little more energy if she lost a pound or two. Not that she was really overweight but she had to keep an eye on herself. Obviously no one else was going to bother to. But tonight she needed to build up her strength.

She put the tray on the table and went over to the mirror. No, she didn't look well at all. She'd have to be careful. She applied herself to the contents of the tray, decided that even an appeal to Sue would probably go unregarded, and filled herself a hot water bottle at eight thirty to assist her through what she knew would be a distraught and sleepless night.

Julian Frayn crossed the road, briefcase in hand, and entered his house. He went straight up the stairs to the attic and stood in the doorway of his wife's makeshift study. Kate, dishevelled and unaware of his scrutiny, nibbled her top lip and scribbled furiously. After some seconds, he crossed the room and peered over her shoulder. 'Going well?'

She started and grinned up at him. 'Oh, golly, what's the time? I suppose it's heartless to say it's been a good day, but once the Inspector and his satellite had left, I thought of a way to get this chapter moving on. It's been stuck for a week. How're things going with you? Are you back for good?'

Frayn ticked off the answers on his fingers. 'It's half past six. I don't think Sarah would expect you to stop working. I've had a most interesting day and I'm back till nine in the morning when there's a staff meeting. I won't quote Mrs Barstow's unoriginal comments about life having to go on. I will say that, though I was probably fonder of Sarah than most of the staff, the fact that she ate her last meal on this earth at breakfast-time today doesn't mean that I'm going to follow suit as a mark of respect.'

Taking this as a reproach because no meal was in preparation, Kate leapt up and began to apologise. He placed a finger over her lips and executed a Victorian bow. 'Madam, allow me to wine and dine you. I'm not sure whether we've earned it or just need it, but we're eating out in either event. We'll drive over to Bradford, where hardly anyone knows us and then no one will join us to see how much we can tell them. Go and wash the ink off your nose.'

She grinned and obeyed, reappearing in less than a quarter of an hour fit to grace the grandest of dinner tables. Her husband was standing in the hall at the telephone. He covered the mouthpiece and mimed appreciation of her appearance. 'Can you make instant coffee without ruining that get-up? I won't be a minute but there's something I need to have a word with Geoff about. Then I'll shower and drink the coffee and we'll go.'

'You're very conscientious under all that flippancy,' she observed, and disappeared obediently into the kitchen.

His quick-changing ability rivalled hers and, in ten minutes, he presented himself, handsome in dark suit and white shirt, his hair damp and extra curly. She handed him his cup. 'You haven't polished your shoes and I can tell from your face that you didn't get your own way with Geoff. You've only been in a few minutes. Couldn't it wait until things were back to normal? You are a slave to duty.'

'No, it couldn't, and it was because I was being a slave to my duties as a husband, when I should have been in school, that I haven't got an eight-hundred-strong alibi for

149

this morning's little fracas. Come on, woman, I'm starving.'

Four hours later, having seen him dispose of an excellent meal, and knowing from the relaxed arm across her shoulders that he was only healthily tired, Kate felt free to put the question which had occupied her mind for much of the evening. She wriggled round to face him. 'Ju, who do you think did it? Do you really think it was a member of staff?'

He answered her without a pause. 'Yes, I think it must have been, for all sorts of practical reasons and because I have a sort of gut feeling about it. But I can't tell you which one.'

She leaned her head on his shoulder. 'Did you have a rotten day, really?'

He appeared surprised at the question. 'No, not personally. Of course, the whole thing was a shock, but it caused some very interesting and uncharacteristic reactions.'

Her eyebrows shot up but then she relaxed and smiled. 'If I didn't know you better, I'd say you were only an observer of life and never got involved in it enough for it to hurt you. Whose uncharacteristic reactions were you watching?'

'I had a pretty unusual chat with young White for one.'

'The PE man?'

'Yes. He's an irritating young brute who spends most of his free time sniping at the head, the deputies except Maynard, the rest of the staff and most of the rest of the world. He's very fair and painstaking with the children, though. Anyway, it turns out that he can't have any. His wife's fertile and it looks as though he isn't. He's been trying to bolster up his manhood by being a fine physical specimen. Maybe that explains his bond with Geoff.'

'But he's small and slight.'

'Maybe, but they don't come much fitter. White's very bitter about Sarah begrudging him time out of school for hospital tests. He found her unsympathetic and her questions rude and humiliating. He was asking me about adoption.'

She stiffened. 'You? What did he expect you to know about it?'

'Nothing first hand. I didn't say anything about us, but one of the sixth-formers I take a great interest in is adopted.'

Kate nodded. 'You mean Valerie? I know Mrs Kelsey. She's a librarian at the branch in town. She's taken a lot of trouble to track down information for me from time to time. I gather they haven't exactly had an easy ride with her.'

'I'm sure they haven't but it's been very successful. They've been an ideal couple to bring her up. They each had a career of their own and weren't trying to live through her, and she isn't their blood child so they weren't looking for their own talents and abilities to appear in her or putting pressure on her to fulfil their own failed ambitions. Yet they've provided a professional, cultured background. The result is, they've given a very talented but difficult girl an ideal environment to develop in and begin to achieve her own immense potential. Kevin was getting quite keen on the idea when I left him,'

'But he might find he'd adopted a potential moron with two left feet.'

Startled by the expression this remark brought to his face, she was brought up short. 'Julian, is this what you want for us?'

His mouth twisted. 'What? Saddle you with a potential moron with two left feet. No, I wasn't talking about us.'

She looked away. 'No. I see.' Scrambling to her feet, she switched on the radio.

By the time Browne dismissed him, Kevin White realised it was too late to pick up Chris from the shop. She'd heard the news and would have understood his non-appearance. The Mini had made an initial protest when he started her up but then she had chugged home safely. It had been a sedentary day, apart from the exercises with which he had passed the time at the police station. Comparing this with the amount of energy he usually expended, he wondered why he felt exhausted.

He found Chris watching the television news which was just passing from matters of national to matters of local importance. Two trays, laden with meat and salad, sat on the kitchen table by the back door.

'Do you want these bringing through?' he called.

'Yes, let's eat in front of the telly. They're just reporting your murder.'

She didn't seem upset. He dutifully bore the trays to the settee and settled himself beside her, but the report on Miss Bland's demise was brief and as he prepared to watch, it finished.

Chris asked with interest, 'Did you see the body, Kev?'

He realised she was avid for drama rather than concerned for his sensibilities and was reluctant both to satisfy her morbid curiosity and to recall the events of the day. All he really wanted to do was sleep. He leaned back against the Dralon cushion, and, for the first time, questioned their desire for a child. He wanted one and he wanted to gratify Chris's desire for one but, thinking over his conversation with Frayn, he asked himself what sort of parents they would make. She was still waiting for an answer and he gave her one she was not expecting.

'I haven't seen Miss Bland today, either alive or dead, which is a good thing, considering that I predicted her murder, exactly as it happened, in the hearing of almost the whole staff. I'd just opened a letter telling me she hadn't recommended me for the Birley course. I felt like doing it.'

Her eyes rounded as he explained his position. She heard him out, absorbed what he told her and began to look alarmed. 'You mean, you're a real suspect?'

'Well, I am in the sense that I just about had the opportunity and that I didn't get on with her any better than the rest of the staff did, but I don't think I'm top of the Inspector's list.'

She nodded, then switched her attention to the last morsel of red beef. As she chewed, an unpleasant thought struck her. 'Kev, will it make a difference, you being mixed up in a murder case? You know, with the adoption people.'

'Oh, hell! I hadn't got round to thinking about that.

At least, I'd only thought that now the old bat's out of the way I'd be able to get to the interviews without the damned nosy questions and hassle about time off that she gave me when I was getting the fertility checks done.' He flushed painfully at the memory of the double humiliation, then added, attempting to reassure her, 'It can't make any difference once they find out who did it.'

'No. Just so long as they do.'

Glenys Freebourne's spirits sank lower as she saw her husband's battered Beetle parked outside the house. So much for the ten minutes she'd been hoping to steal with a cup of tea and her feet up before preparing the family meal. Now she'd have to get on with it straight away, whilst listening to a recital of the injustices done in this afternoon's court session to one or other of Ted's probationers. Not that she wasn't interested in his work, but she felt a pressing need for a short space to sort out the events of her own day.

For once, he seemed to sense her need to unwind and talk. Sprawled in the shabby armchair, one leg hooked over the end of the more frayed arm, he reached to pull her down on the other. He was still wearing his duffel coat. 'I've already put the kettle on. I hear it's all been happening at your place today. Spill!' He employed what he believed to be the teen-age idiom, in the hope that it made his charges feel he could communicate with them, and often forgot to revert to a more normal vocabulary until Neville's sneers reminded him.

His wife leaned against the lumpy chairback and regaled him with her version of the day's events, omitting only their son's misdemeanours and making much of her colleagues' fury at the indignities to which they had been subjected at the police station. Her grin broadened. 'I had a maternal visitation this morning, so, as she was on the premises at the relevant time, she got the same treatment. A bit more than she'd bargained for.'

Ted's face lit up with delighted astonishment. 'Marched down to the station and divested of her modesty? Oh, joy! What did she want, anyway?'

'What does she always want? To tell me that Mel passed her house last night with a youngster who "didn't look a nice boy at all", to repeat that whilst I keep bees, the children run riot. To suggest that one daughter to dominate should have sufficed me as it did her. To make it clear that Nev and the twins were an unfortunate superfluity, due mainly to your reckless lust and my failure to control it. She has rather illogical ideas about maternal responsibility. It's my fault that my daughter's a slut but it's not her fault that I am.'

She paused to accept the cup of tea that Ted had poured and they sipped without speaking, to the beat of raucous music from the room above. Ted reached out and took her hand. 'You're not and Mel's not, so she's wrong on both counts.' As he drained his cup, another idea struck him. 'Hey! do you remember when Mel applied to join the civil service and the Bland woman refused to give her a reference?'

Glenys Freebourne nodded. 'Yes, she said Mel wasn't up to it and wouldn't enjoy it.'

Ted refilled their cups. 'I was as mad as hell about it at the time, but after I'd thought about it I decided she was probably quite right. There was no silencing your ma, though. She was screaming blue murder against Miss Bland. Perhaps the Inspector would be interested to hear about that. Go and help the police with their enquiries and you might really get her off your back.'

Carol Weston glowered at the meal her husband had waiting for her. She wrinkled her nose as she removed at least thirty calories' worth of skin from her chicken leg and moved her salad away from the generous blob of mayonnaise. He hid his chagrin and left her to open the conversation.

'I'm not so much later than usual,' was her offering. 'It wouldn't have taken me long to cook a proper meal.'

He still tried to appease her. 'Well, rumours were rife. Obviously, they couldn't all be true, but I knew you must be having a pretty bad day and wouldn't feel like cooking.'

She capitulated ungraciously, pulling out a chair and sitting at the table. 'Well, since it's here we may as well eat it.' Neither the memory nor the recapitulation of the morning's events spoiled her appetite. She ate quickly and related the facts with equanimity. Her husband listened, wearing the hang-dog look that most people had who spent long in her company.

'What happens now?' he asked her. 'I suppose Maynard's in charge until something permanent's settled.'

She snorted. 'If he hasn't cracked up completely before we reopen. He's behaving like a menopausal maiden aunt. He practically passed out when we went in and found her. I had to ring the police and get everything organised.'

'I'm sure you coped without him. Do you go in as usual tomorrow?'

She finished eating and pushed away her plate. 'School's not in session till we have the police say-so but there's a staff meeting with the dishy Sergeant Hunter as an ex-officio attender. Maynard didn't have the courtesy to invite me but I'll be there. I shall go on doing my job as I did under Miss Bland. I can't see the governors leaving Maynard with the reins for long. Are we going out for a drink?'

'If you still feel like it.'

She looked surprised. 'Why shouldn't I? I don't see why someone settling a score with Sarah Bland should make me less thirsty.'

In spite of being kept past the usual time, there was still an hour for Meg Rivers to work in her kitchen before her husband was due home. She needed the time. She had intended to make a meal from the results of a couple of demonstration lessons and when the Inspector allowed her to leave, the shops were all shut. In accordance with the principles she instilled into her pupils, her own freezer and store cupboard were well stocked with the raw materials to produce a good meal in just such an emergency. A survey of her herb and spice rack had inspired a Mexican casserole which was simmering in the oven. Now she was mashing slightly overripe bananas, whilst pieces of plain chocolate melted over a pan of hot water on the stove. She'd mix them together and then fold in cream to get a marbled effect that would show through if she served the sweet in the thin Swedish glasses. There was no need to drop her standards just because she'd had an awkward day. The Swedish glass caused her to get out the lace mats that they usually saved for high days and holidays. They might produce an idea for a suitable starter before she heard the car coming up the drive. The elegance of the lace suggested candles, and, whether or not they were the source of inspiration, she remembered the vol au vent cases in the top of the freezer. Perhaps the sauce for the filling could come out of a jar, just for once, then she'd have time to bath and change.

By the time the car drew up on the loose gravel in front of the double garage, she was fresh and elegant in a holly green sheath, ready to pour the sherry. The large man who came in a couple of minutes later seemed in need of it and disposed of it speedily.

'What the hell's going on, Meg?' he asked her. 'I gave a lift to young Martin, next door, and he says his friend from your place has had a holiday today because someone's been murdered. He did have the consideration to assure me that he didn't think it was you. I wasn't sure whether he was telling me that you weren't the victim or weren't the culprit.' His gaze registered the glass, lace and candles. 'Oh, God, we haven't got people coming?'

'No.' She refilled his glass. 'But I can do with a civilising influence tonight even if you can't. Yes, we did have a murder done this morning. Victim, our revered headmistress; scene of crime, her inner sanctum; murder weapon, a weird but attractive model cat that she keeps on her desk.'

'My God! It isn't funny, Meg.'

She fought the rising hysteria. 'Isn't it? You should hear about the funny day I've had, the third degree from two handsome policemen, a striptease down at the station and everybody desperately trying to pretend the silly woman didn't deserve it. I've cooked an extra special supper to

156

mark the event.' She leaned against the imposing Victorian mantelpiece and shook with mirthless laughter.

His face as white as hers, her husband took a step towards her, restrained himself, and, fists clenched, turned on his heel. 'You callous cow! You can eat it yourself. I'm going out.' The dining-room door slammed, followed in succession by the front door and that of the grey Mercedes. There was a pause of more than a minute before the engine purred.

By then, she was herself again and shrugged her shoulders at the faint sound. She didn't fancy the food either but she wouldn't clear it away. If he drank himself into a better mood he might come back and want it. She took off her dress, replacing it with a shabby dressing-gown, switched on the iron in the little laundry off the kitchen and began to attack the frills on one of his dress shirts.

Frayn's phone call found Maynard frowning over his third form's rearrangement of the map of France. He felt he might have accustomed himself to their improvements if there had been any measure of agreement about the novel siting of the various features he had required his pupils to mark on their outline maps. He thanked his stars that he had decided to provide at least these, otherwise the French would have been astonished to find their coastline replanned for good measure. Not unwilling to be interrupted, he took the receiver from his middle daughter who had left the ironing board to get it.

He listened to Frayn's importunate voice and sought to soothe him. 'I know the references are urgent, Julian. No, I must see them but by all means do a rough draft of those two if you've time. We'll mull over them after the meeting tomorrow. I shouldn't get too steamed up, though. Their papers will get both of them in without our recommendations. No one's going to keep either of those two down. Thanks for taking the trouble. See you tomorrow.'

He replaced the receiver, cast his eyes to heaven, then winked at Vicky who was painstakingly pressing his best shirt in preparation for his first day as acting head. The least academic of his three daughters, she had left Heath Lees last year to work in the local bank. Now that she was out of it all, and because her lack of scholarship was compensated for by a generous share of common sense and discretion, he allowed himself the luxury, now and again, of expressing his feelings to her on school matters.

'Once Julian gets his teeth into sixth-form business there's no tearing it away from him.' Strains could be heard from upstairs of a flute exercise being assiduously and more than competently repeated. 'It's a good job he isn't musical or he might be trying to take over Joanna. Fortunately, he's practically tone deaf, though he'd never admit it, so he contents himself with telling her not to waste her talent and telling me not to let her. She's all the better for both of us taking no notice of him.'

Vicky adjusted the iron's thermostat. 'I thought you liked Mr Frayn.'

'I do, very much, but he does get bees in his bonnet about what he thinks is best for people.'

Maynard heard his wife coming in from the garden, her arms full of more dry clothes from the line, and by mutual consent, the conversation between father and daughter ceased. Frances was not insensitive and knew her husband's ostentatious resumption of his marking and her daughter's studious attention to the tucked blouse now on the ironing board had brought to an end some exchange between them from which she was excluded. She knew, too, that she forfeited her husband's confidences about his work by being too ready to take up cudgels on his behalf in situations he felt were best left to work themselves out. She was impatient with his diffident manner of dealing with people whom she thought took advantage of him. She would probably have been surprised and impressed at seeing his firm discipline in the classroom.

She knew they were now too set in their ways to change and merely beamed her gratitude to Vicky. 'One of the sweetest scents in the world is that of clothes freshly ironed by someone else,' she remarked as she dumped her burden on top of the basket already half full of crumpled garments. 'Leave that, now,' she told her daughter, 'and go and get washed for supper. Tell Jo to do the same and then she can lay the table. By the time Helen's back from gym club, I should have the meal ready.' She glanced at the table where her husband had created a similar chaos to the one on his office desk. 'Can you spare a corner of that for us to eat at?' she asked him with a grin. 'You'd better not get Miss Bland's desk into that state or the governors will have you forcibly removed.'

Maynard was cheerfully removing the worst of the mess until she paused in the doorway. 'Not that it will come to that. By lunch-time tomorrow, the Weston woman will have made her takeover bid and you will be meekly functioning as her secretary.'

She regretted the words immediately. Countless times she had tried to goad him into decisive action against people she thought usurped his authority, and all she managed to do was to undermine further his confidence and antagonise him. She saw his mouth harden and tried to take the sting out of her words by rumpling his hair. When he made no response, she slipped into the chair beside him. 'I'm sorry, Geoff. The woman riles me and makes me want to defend you. Throw those books into that box to keep them together. I'll wash up after supper and you can go out for a ten-miler. You can run today out of your system, the murder, the headship, the redoubtable Weston and your overbearing wife.'

Chapter 10

When Hunter set off for Maynard's first staff meeting, the day had not yet decided which mood of autumn it would reflect. He paused at his gate and looked up to a sky covered in unlikely cloud markings, as though Fliss, with a giant white crayon, had scribbled aggressive straight strokes across it. He decided it wouldn't rain and set off to walk the short distance to the school.

Along his own road and the adjoining ones the gardens were trim and colourful but presently he came to the housing estate which bordered the school and formed about a third of its catchment area. Here he observed all degrees of order and disorder in juxtaposition. Gleaming new paint nestled up against cracked and peeling doors and neglected wildernesses threatened to overrun tiny, carefully tended lawns and borders. Over one low wall, a coy gnome grinned at him whilst its companion concentrated on catching a non-existent fish, and, at a corner where the angle between the houses had allocated a double share of land to one of them, a few square feet of newly dug dark earth on the edge of a sea of dandelion and dock indicated a new tenant's stout intention.

Using the zebra crossing, Hunter reached the school gate and walked up the drive. The buildings had that air of being a mistake which belongs to all purpose-built constructions that are, temporarily, not serving that purpose. He walked past the main block, making his way first to the Head's study, entering it from the corridor after knocking. Maynard was not there but someone was moving about in the office next door. He noticed that the furniture had been moved around so that a filing cabinet covered the stains on the carpet but obscured the wall board with its array of notices and timetables. The desk now faced the window, as though Maynard could not bring himself to assume the position in which Miss Bland had died. The bookcase beside the desk had been cleared on to the floor to make room for the more essential of Maynard's accoutrements.

After a minute or so, Mrs Weston appeared, unannounced, in the connecting doorway. 'I just wondered who was poking around in here,' she observed accusingly. Then, appalled by the devastation the temporary Head had achieved in so short a time, she moved in uninvited. 'My God! I'd better put this lot to rights whilst it's still possible to find anything.'

'Do you know where I can find Mr Maynard?'

She answered him with her back to him, busily restoring order. 'Try his own office. He's probably collecting more rubbish to create chaos with in here.'

Hunter left to follow up the suggestion, speculating with relish on the confrontation that would result if Mrs Weston's surmise were accurate. He grinned broadly when he met Maynard, struggling to open the fire doors whilst balancing a dozen or so dog-eared files against his chest. He helped him through, then requested that the meeting should begin promptly at nine, even if there were latecomers.

Strolling along the corridor towards the staff room he encountered Frayn emerging from the men's cloakroom and tackled him on the subject of his approach to Keats with his first-year class. 'Tim was sitting there,' he complained, 'chanting the lines with no conception whatsoever of their meaning.'

Frayn smiled. 'Of course he hasn't. It's not relevant to the lad at the moment. He's only interested in the fast-moving here and now. When he's mature enough for the there and then, he'll take it from the bookself in his mind and have another look at it. I'm stocking his mental library.'

161

Hunter had known Frayn would have an answer. He allowed the English master to open the staff room door for him and usher him in. They interrupted an impassioned speech on an aspect of the previous day, hitherto unmentioned.

'You know this authority. They'll pull back the lost day from somewhere. Well, if they dock it from the holidays as an occasional day, I'll be straight on to the union. We reported in for duty, didn't we? And, heaven knows, we didn't exactly sneak home early. It was nearly half past six when I got my tea!'

Kevin White paused for breath and noticed Hunter's arrival. 'Good morning, Sergeant.' They grinned at each other amiably and the young man who had been White's captive audience drifted across to another group of staff engaged in desultory argument about the purpose of education. It seemed to Hunter that the lofty subject held little interest for them and that they were quoting formulae and opinions from past debates to fill in an awkward wait. White, drawn by the smell of coffee, joined them. 'I'm satisfied,' he declared, reaching for a cup, 'if I can prevent the horrible brats from killing one another until it's time to return them to their equally horrible parents.'

Maynard came in, consulted his watch, seated himself and opened the file he had brought with him. Acknowledging the signal, the staff settled themselves round him and waited expectantly. Mrs Weston, Hunter noted, had been left behind; first round to Maynard.

Browne, too, paused at his gate before setting off for his morning's work, in his case to admire a cluster of Princess Elizabeths, growing tall against the fence. It was towards the end of their season and many of their blooms were overblown, the petals a bleached pink with papery brown edges like discarded, crumpled tissues. Each bush was still producing a few buds, though, of sharp, rich pink, the petals tightly overlapped, only the tips curled slightly outwards to promise a full unfolding.

Dean, waiting beside the car at the gate, opened the passenger door, perhaps as a gentle hint that Browne should stop his musings if he wanted to catch his train. Climbing in quickly, Browne contemplated his programme for the day. He wasn't quite sure what he was hoping to learn from Mr and Mrs Bland or whether they could help the enquiry at all. He didn't really think the answer to the puzzle lay in London but he couldn't neglect to see them. Besides, there would be questions they would want to ask him. His touch with the relatives of the victims in his cases was reputed to be sure and sympathetic. He could only suppose that his ability to help them was in direct proportion to the distaste and discomfort he felt at having to intrude on their privacy in their grief.

He enjoyed renewing his acquaintance with the bustle and noise of St Pancras, then clattering via the Northern and District lines to Wimbledon Park but his spirits sank as he neared his destination. A preliminary phone call to the local station had informed him that Mr Bland had suffered a further heart attack during the night and the distracted woman who admitted him to the respectable villa at the end of its cul-de-sac looked in need of whatever succour he could offer. He had not been certain of finding Mrs Bland at home and it soon proved that her departure to the hospital was imminent.

Even so she offered him coffee and an attempted smile. Feeling that coffee would benefit her more than himself, Browne accepted and soon her teeth were chattering against Royal Albert china in the Old Country Roses design.

'I don't really think you'll be able to interview my husband, Inspector,' she told him worriedly.

He assured her that was not his intention.

'I'm sure I'll do all I can to help you discover who did this dreadful thing. I can't believe it. Who could have wanted to harm Sarah?'

Browne forbore to list the names that occurred to him, but wondered if, perhaps, Miss Bland had not provoked in London the animosity she had in Cloughton.

163

'Do you know,' he asked her, 'if any friend or acquaintance has been from here to Yorkshire to visit Sarah recently?'

She shook her head. 'Someone could have done. She doesn't tell us what she does. A few weeks ago, I met her in a coffee house in town. I didn't know she was up and I think she was intending to go back without coming to see us. She was with a gentleman friend.' Her voice flattened. 'He was quicker thinking than Sarah. She was never devious. He said, "Oh, dear, you've spoilt her surprise. She was going to drop in this evening before her flying visit was over." '

Keeping his voice level, Browne enquired, 'Did she introduce him to you?'

'Well, of course she did. She does have some manners. But I can't remember his name. Something Irish, I think.'

'Was he an Irishman?'

'He didn't sound it. He had the sort of voice that goes with the old school tie.'

'Did she have a lot of men friends?'

Mrs Bland looked surprised. 'I've never seen her with a man before, except to do with her work. She looked really happy with him, I'll say that. Sarah didn't manage to be happy very often.'

Browne produced a card and wrote on it. 'If you remember the man's name, could I trouble you to ring this number? It would be very helpful.'

She nodded, her mind on other things, and was silent for some seconds as she finished her coffee. 'Sarah forgot her camera when she called that evening. The film was finished and her father developed it for her. It's his hobby. Perhaps, if you're going back to Cloughton, you could – Oh, dear.' She stopped, aghast. 'I was going to ask you to pass them on to her. I still haven't taken it in.'

'Don't worry, Mrs Bland. You're besieged with problems at the moment. I'm not surprised your mind's rejecting some of them. I wonder if you'd mind fetching the photographs all the same? They might help us.'

She produced them without comment and he scanned them quickly. Presently, he drew out one of the prints from the set and handed it to her, eyebrows raised. It showed a relaxed Sarah Bland smiling up into the face of a well set up, silver-haired man.

'Oh, yes,' the woman agreed. 'That's the man I was telling you about.'

Suddenly, the telephone rang and she started and jumped up. 'It'll be the hospital.' She disappeared into the hall, reappearing almost immediately, a coat over her arm. 'My husband's awake and asking for me. I'm afraid I'll have to ask you to go.'

Browne said the proper things regarding her husband's recovery and a speedy conclusion to the case before she drove away. They hadn't mentioned the inquest or the funeral arrangements but, for the moment, she was more concerned for the husband who was still alive. He had pocketed the interesting snapshot and examined it for some seconds before setting off to walk the short distance back to Wimbledon Park station. The face seemed faintly familiar but he couldn't place it. Perhaps the name would click into his mind if he didn't worry at it.

He left it to come at its leisure whilst he looked for somewhere to have lunch before the afternoon train to Bradford. It didn't, but as he waited for his coffee he fished out the snapshot again, examining portions of it through a small but powerful magnifying glass. Miss Bland's companion had something pinned to his lapel, a small oblong disc with writing on it. It looked like the sort of name tag worn by the attenders at conferences or courses. He bent closer to the glass and made out BR at the beginning of the first word and S at the end of the second. The words underneath, in bigger letters, were magnified clearly: 'CLOUGHTON, YORKS'. He'd better get back quickly and show the picture around there.

Browne's first port of call on his arrival home was the police station. He put his head into the incident room where all was bustle and activity and where he was informed that Hunter was looking for him. Browne was not surprised to hear from his house-to-house team that the school had been besieged with mysterious strangers yesterday, tall and short, dark and fair, sneaking suspiciously or running in fear and most of them carrying strange objects which were probably vicious weapons. One such concerned a red-haired man with a limp, who had crossed the school car park, his hands dripping blood, and disappeared down a snicket that led straight to the shopping centre. Browne wondered whether the extreme shakiness of the witness's signature was due to DT or extreme old age. He enquired of Dean, who had produced this information.

Dean sniggered. 'I asked her why she hadn't reported to us at once, sir. She said she was used to such carryings on at that place and had had to learn to live with it.'

Browne offered a word of encouragement to the men faced with the tedious following up of these unlikely reports, then produced a charming smile for the young woman who was conferring with the constable on duty at the reception desk. 'You'd save my life, Karen, if you produced a cup of tea.'

She leapt with alacrity to comply with the request and he retired to his office, to which Hunter arrived before the tea. He seemed pregnant with news and Browne took pity on him.

'Get anything useful this morning?'

Hunter shrugged. 'Not much that gets the case any further but plenty of melodrama.'

Browne had to wait for his account of it as Karen's knock heralded the delivery of the promised tea. There were two wrapped chocolate biscuits, perhaps her apology for her dalliance with the constable on the desk. Browne drank thirstily whilst Hunter removed the silver wrapper from a biscuit and began to fold it into complicated convolutions. Satisfied with the work of art he had created, he continued his tale. 'It all went quite smoothly at first. They agreed to reopen as normal tomorrow. They worked out

166

ways of letting people know, evening paper, local radio and so on. Maynard told them the authority had granted a supply teacher indefinitely – or at least until another appointment can be made. Frayn was concerned that Maynard's exam group would be neglected and there was some discussion about that.'

'Did the resourceful Mrs Weston supply the solution to all these problems?'

'She wasn't there. Apparently Maynard gave her some work to do and told her to stay in the office.'

'Bravo! Then he'll probably cope with everything else. Carry on.'

'There was some talk about what line to take with the children, how to answer their questions about the enquiry. Some staff thought parents would refuse to send their children in until an arrest is made.'

'We shall have to set them a good example,' Browne interrupted smugly. 'Come on lad, I'm waiting for this melodrama.'

'Well, after a while, the awful Stafford got up and stumbled out. No one said or did anything. After all, she might have just been going to the loo, though most people would have done it with a bit less fuss. When, after five minutes, she hadn't returned I saw Meg Rivers's eyes meet Maynard's. She raised her eyebrows, Maynard gave an almost imperceptible nod and Rivers crept out. She was back in short order to say that Stafford was out cold in the cloakroom and she suspected an overdose.'

'What fun!' Browne commented mildly.

'I made a cursory examination, Maynard got an ambulance and the meeting broke up in chaos. She hadn't made a proper job of it. Didn't mean to, of course. Pity she had to be asleep and miss all the fuss she caused. Anyway, they're keeping her in hospital overnight and Maynard is demanding a second supply.'

'Demanding, is he? He's coming on. What a pity I took the day off and missed all the excitement. Would you mind eating that biscuit, now you've demolished the wrapper?'

As Hunter chewed obediently, Browne described his own doings and produced his photograph. Hunter peered at it for almost a minute but was unable to identify the man.

'Where do we look for him?'

'I think we'll begin by asking Mr Maynard.'

Maynard looked weary as he opened the door to them, but he welcomed them into the dusty muddle behind him and called to his wife to produce coffee. Browne relaxed in the armchair Maynard cleared for him but Hunter could not be comfortable when such confusion dominated the pleasant, high-ceilinged Victorian room. The kettle must have been boiling, for Frances appeared after a couple of minutes with a dainty tray. Both policemen had expected a worn-out-looking female as untidy as her husband and were surprised to find her small, slight and neat with an alert expression and friendly smile. She made Browne think of a domesticated sparrow.

Looking round at the disorder, Browne saw that Frances Maynard was surveying it too, with a deprecating grin. He suddenly saw it afresh as the result of two lively-minded people and their offspring, ruefully cheerful about having their days too full to fit in their domestic chores. The untidiness was the impedimenta of their interests, lying handy for taking up again, a flute and several recorders in cases, books in piles, showing much evidence of having been consulted, a typewriter and piles of notes and a playscript with one role heavily underlined.

Having watched them dispose of the coffee, Frances rose. 'Do you want to talk to Geoff on his own?'

'Not at all. I just want to know if either of you recognise the man in this photograph.'

She reached for it, glanced at it and drew in her breath, sharply. 'That's Brendan Rivers, Meg's husband.'

Browne rose and motioned to Hunter to follow suit. 'In that case,' he told Frances, taking the picture back and returning it to his pocket, 'we'll thank you for your hospitality and ask the rest of our questions at the Rivers' house.'

As Browne made to climb back into the car, Hunter hesitated. 'Is it worth moving the car, sir, when they live in the same road?'

Browne laughed and beckoned him in. 'They live in the same road, Jerry, but not in the same world. Between number ten and number forty-two we pass from the merely respectable through the desirable to the splendid. The gardens get increasingly more extensive and it's well over a mile.'

Hunter was convinced and climbed in. 'I wonder whether Mrs Rivers is in for a nasty shock,' he remarked as he tried to fold his legs into the available space.

'Our having the photograph might shock her,' Browne allowed, 'but when we asked her if she knew who B might be, she tipped her bag at my feet and she isn't normally a clumsy woman.'

Hunter was not to be outdone. 'I did notice that B was one of the initials on the letter she dropped. Another one was M, though, so they might have been hers.'

One point seven miles further up the road, Browne signalled and turned left.

Hunter looked surprised. 'I thought it was straight on.'

'We've arrived.'

'You mean, this is their drive? Jeepers!' He stared around him in awe. 'Why on earth does she teach?'

'She likes kids, I think. I'm grateful anyway. She taught Virginia when she was in the third year. Ginny came home one night and announced that Mrs Rivers had said you were not a complete person if another person still had responsibility for your domestic arrangements by the time you were fourteen. She's organised her own laundry and room cleaning ever since.'

Hunter chuckled. 'Do boys do her subject as well?' he asked hopefully. Then he was silenced as a magnificent house came into view.

Browne was more struck by the gardens. They displeased him. He found something almost obscene about earth and grass and flowers being used to convey opulence. He felt an urge to disarrange things a little, to fray the edges of the neatly hemmed lawns. Instead, wondering which of the childless pair was responsible for the orders to the gardener, he placed his thumb on the bell-push in its gleaming brass surround.

It was the sort of house that should have had a butler and it seemed strange when Meg Rivers opened the door herself. Her voice was welcoming but her expression guarded as she invited them in and offered them coffee. Hunter looked horrified until reassured that, this time, Browne was going to refuse. She took them into a sitting-room that looked like an illustration out of *Homes and Gardens* and stood facing them.

They apologised for disturbing her. 'We need to speak to your husband. Is he in?'

'To Brendan?' She sank suddenly into a cavernous chair and waved them to seats across the room. 'He's not due back for a couple of hours, I'm afraid. He's out with a client. I can't tell you where you can contact him but the firm might. It's Dale, Rivers and Greenwood of Bradford.'

Browne smiled. 'How very topographical. I think it will suffice if you ask him to get in touch with us as soon as he gets back.'

He watched her suddenly come to a decision. 'You know about Brendan and Sarah, don't you?'

'So you did too,' Browne countered.

She nodded. 'I didn't do away with her to get him back. That would have been about as effective as swatting the mosquito that bit you and expecting the others to leave you alone.'

Browne's face registered nothing.

'I knew he'd got someone again but I didn't know it was Sarah. I've been reaching that conclusion by degrees.'

Browne knew that sharpness or sympathy would stem the flow of this uncharacteristic confession. He asked, tonelessly, 'What made you suspect?'

'Some of the things she seemed to know about him that I hadn't told her. For instance, I missed a parents' evening in the second week of term and she assumed we were going out because it was Bren's birthday. I certainly hadn't mentioned it at school. Then he was so angry because I'd cooked dinner as usual last night despite what had happened. He doesn't usually go on hunger strike to mark the misfortunes of mere acquaintances. His face when I told him the model was the weapon was indescribable. I think he must have given it to her. It dawned on me last night that she acquired it during the week Bren was at his London conference.'

After a few seconds' silence she shook back her hair and resumed her normal brisk manner. They saw that her moment of weakness was over and that they were unlikely to persuade her to reveal more.

'I don't think there's any more I can tell you.'

They accepted the dismissal and took their leave. 'We'll split up now,' Browne directed. 'You go back to the station like a good chap. Poke your nose into the incident room and jolly them along, then hang about in case our friend turns up earlier than expected.'

'Do we suspect him?'

'We suspect everybody. When we've had a good look at him, we'll see if he matches up with any of the mysterious strangers whom the local populace say were hanging about the place yesterday.'

'Right, sir. Where will I find you if I need to?'

'I'm going to take my daughter's advice and see what the two prefects on assembly duty yesterday have to say. I'll be at the Kelsey house at Shaw Dean.'

As Browne walked up the path through the tiny garden, Carol Kelsey caught sight of him through the window. She came to the door shaking her head. 'Virginia isn't here. I haven't seen her tonight.' She stood back for him to enter and took him into the living-room.

'It's Valerie I wanted to see,' he explained. 'I need to ask her a few questions about yesterday.'

Mrs Kelsey's friendly manner became frostbitten. 'What's Valerie supposed to know about it?'

171

Browne cursed himself for his careless approach. When Mrs Kelsey had first taken her adopted daughter in as a foster child she had not had reason to be pleased to find the police at the door and it had taken years of Virginia's uninhibited friendliness to convince her that she came to the house because she enjoyed Valerie's company and not to supervise on her father's behalf. He hastened to reassure her.

'I'm here because Ginny suggested it. Valerie was one of the prefects on duty yesterday and as she's extremely observant, I need to know what she can tell me. I'd like you to be there whilst I'm talking to her to make sure I don't upset her.'

She was mollified but still doubtful. 'I'll call her down.'

Feet thudded in response to the call and Valerie burst into the room. She smiled at Browne and he realised with a shock that in the last few months she had become almost beautiful. She had the sort of face that she was growing into. The features which had appeared heavy and aggressive in the child, had become, in the budding woman, striking and effective. He realised that, like him, she was remembering their previous formal interviews. He had been a sergeant then, less experienced and less wise. She had been angry and unhappy and dumpy, the muddy skin marred with angry eruptions and the lank dark hair inclined to greasiness. Though even then there had been an alert dark glance that had redeemed her. Her beauty now was not merely that of a pleasing exterior but of an intimidating intelligence shining through it. For the first time he understood Frayn's crusade for her. He began his questions.

'Virginia says you were on assembly duty yesterday. What exactly does that involve?'

She perched on a chair arm. 'There are two of us. We just have to make sure everything flows smoothly. We stop people talking before they come in and hurry along anyone who's late.'

'How smoothly did everything flow yesterday?'

'Fairly, except for Miss Bland not turning up.'

'Did people realise she should have been there?'

She nodded. 'Oh, yes. The high-ups each have their own day for leading prayers. We knew it was hers. Mind you, she's been held up before when she's had a visitor and someone's had to substitute for her but it was obvious yesterday that the platform party was waiting for her and puzzled that there hadn't been a message.'

Browne made a quick note. 'Anything else?'

'Miss Stafford wasn't there. Miss Rogers brought her form in and stood with them. Mrs Rivers's form came in without anybody but it didn't matter because they're sixth. Freebie's lot, Mrs Freebourne's third form, were on their own and they chattered and shuffled until Mr Maynard glared at them. Then there was this great long wait and Mr Chandler played the same bit of organ music about three times over. You'd have thought he could have improvised a bit, wouldn't you? Then Mr Frayn came in a bit late. He didn't take a hymn book from the table at the front. I was glad. He usually picks a choir copy with music in and tries to sing the tenor line in a high reedy voice, with his book held high like a Messiah soloist rendering "Every Valley". I wish he wouldn't. It makes the little ones turn round and giggle and we have to stop them. Yesterday he just sang the tune and two of the kids even found that funny. I had to send them to stand at the front. One of them was Sergeant Hunter's little boy. Mr Frayn left before the hymn finished.'

'What did you make of that?'

'Nothing really. He often leaves before the service is over, especially if there's an Old Testament reading. We asked him about it once. He said he liked fairy stories but not straight after breakfast.'

Browne's pencil had hurried to keep up with Valerie's flow of information. Now he closed his book and left, hoping that Brendan Rivers would be as accurate and succinct a witness.

When he returned to the station, Browne met Hunter in the foyer.

'I was just trying to get you, sir. Rivers arrived about forty minutes ago. He demanded to see you and informed Constable Baker that he'd put off an important engagement to come here and that he'd better find you quickly. He managed a nice compromise between duty-conscious citizen and elevated man of affairs with better things than this to do. We found him an interview room to cool his heels in and told him that Detective Constable Mitchell could spare the time to talk to him in a few minutes. He repeated "Detective Constable?" in the tones that most actresses reserve for Lady Bracknell saying "A handbag?", and they've been closeted together now for half an hour.'

'Which you've spent enjoying the double pleasure of insulting Rivers with a lowly DC and landing Mitchell with an overbearing and conceited witness.'

Hunter had the grace to blush.

Browne finished what he had to say once they were facing each other across his desk. 'Your prospects aren't going to be affected by Mitchell's progress, Jerry, however many short cuts he takes. Why not give him a break and stop spoiling your own job satisfaction by resenting him so much?'

When he received no reply, Browne opened a file and studied its contents. Hunter studied his fingernails in silence until the phone on the desk between them shrilled. Browne gestured to Hunter who answered it. He listened, his lips tightening, then looked up. 'It's Mitchell. He's taken Rivers through yesterday and his alibi for the morning is pretty shaky. Now Rivers insists on speaking to a senior officer.'

Browne frowned. 'Does he now? Tell Mitchell to bring him up here.'

Hunter delivered the message, then rose stiffly. 'I'll wait downstairs,' he announced on his way to the door.

His superior's raised voice stopped him. 'You'll damned well sit over there and notice what I miss. I've had a long day and I'm shattered. I need your wits about me.'

Hunter resumed his seat and less than a minute later, after a tap on the door, Mitchell and his witness entered. The tall, broad-shouldered man seemed less than charmed with the hospitality he had been offered. He stood, glowering, before the Inspector's desk.

Browne, his manner urbane, smiled and offered his hand. 'There was something you wanted to say to me in particular, Mr Rivers?'

Rivers gave the hand a perfunctory shake and glared pointedly at Mitchell, who received a nod from Browne to comply with his visitor's wishes. His surprise rivalled Browne's when the dismissal was softened by a wink from Hunter.

Now Rivers exuded bonhomie. 'I just wanted to discuss the matter with a man of the world, Inspector, rather than with an accusing young copper, still wet behind the ears, who's not as pure as the driven snow himself considering what he tried to deduce from one snapshot of my good self entertaining my wife's headmistress to an innocent lunch.'

'I think his deductions may have been partly based on these,' Browne said, casually producing the briefest of the glamorous undergarments lately returned from the lab. 'And the fact that your "good self" has been identified from the aforementioned snapshot by the girl in Harrods where you made your purchases and by one of Miss Bland's neighbours who witnessed your various comings and goings.'

In the manner of a man modestly disclaiming praise for some small success, Rivers smiled. 'Well, it isn't quite as you think, Inspector. As I said, as one man of affairs, if you'll pardon the pun, to another, I can explain how things were. My relationship with Sarah Bland ended a couple of weeks ago, certainly as far as I was concerned. You're probably wondering what I saw in her.'

'Not really, but I expect you're going to tell me.'

'I think it was her helplessness that appealed to me. She may not have had a soft, feminine appearance but she had her own attraction when she dressed to suit it. She was so gauche and shy, she needed spoiling and squiring before she blossomed. She brought out the gentleman in me.'

Hunter gasped.

'Meg looks decorative but she's so bloody self-sufficient. She's never needed me.'

'She doesn't seem unaware of your philanderings,' Browne put in. 'Perhaps she realised the futility of dependence on you.'

Rivers turned an angry red. 'I'm obviously wasting my valuable time. I've given a signed statement to your office junior. Was there anything else you needed me for?'

He had risen and Browne stood up too.

'Not just now. When we've checked your account of how you spent yesterday morning, we may wish to speak to you again. Please keep yourself available.'

With Dean as an escort, Rivers removed himself with what dignity he could muster. Hunter stood up, turned his chair round and sat down again astride it.

Browne reached for the telephone. 'We'd better have a look at his not very well corroborated alibi. I'll have it sent up.'

Hunter cleared his throat. 'If Mitchell brings it himself, he could add his unofficial comments to his official report. They might be illuminating.'

With a deadpan face and toneless voice, Browne confined his comment to 'Good thinking.'

Chapter 11

Browne decided that it should be Hunter's Friday morning privilege to check Brendan Rivers's alibi. His own responsibility for planning and directing the investigation was lying heavily this morning and he felt he would plan and direct it a great deal better if he had a few hours' respite from it. Attending to some of the routine work which had been piling up in his office during the last two days would allow him to come back fresh to the Bland case and see the various aspects of it in their right proportions.

It was irrational, therefore, he admitted to himself, having despatched Hunter and Mitchell, to feel astonished and resentful when he saw what the petty criminals had been up to during the last two days. Surely they read the newspapers. It was against the rules to take advantage of his preoccupation. What challenge was there in trying to outwit him when he was too busy to pay attention to them?

Shaking his head at his fancies he set to work and when the telephone rang at eleven thirty he had disposed of a satisfactory amount of the backlog. The constable on the desk was diffident about disturbing him.

'It's Mrs Hunter, sir. I was hoping you could tell us where to find the Sergeant or have a word with her yourself.'

Unable to do the former, Browne agreed to speak to Annette who also apologised profusely for interrupting him. 'I just wanted to rescue Tim,' she explained. 'He's rushed off to school in his usual headlong fashion and left his oboe behind. The school band is giving its concert in the market square tomorrow as planned so the last practice is at lunch-time. If Tim misses it Mr Chandler will make him miss the concert too. I was wondering if Jerry could pick up the oboe and drop it into school.'

Browne sighed impatiently. Annette was not the sort of mother to let her son learn from his own mistakes, still less was she a woman to contemplate a three-quarter mile walk herself when her husband had a car. Then he smiled to himself as an idea occurred to him. 'I can't get hold of Jerry unless he happens to drop in,' he told her, 'but I could spare Mitchell for half an hour to help you.' He cut short her protests and renewed apologies. 'I'm not doing it out of the goodness of my heart. Any excuse for a further visit to school at present might push things on a bit further, especially if he can say it's a social call.'

Browne made the necessary arrangements then returned to his papers, whilst a distinctly disgruntled Mitchell set off in the crisp, sunlit morning to rescue his superior's son from the results of his carelessness. Out of courtesy, he visited the head's office but it was in the staff room that he ran Maynard to earth. Mitchell was not sure whether he was demonstrating solidarity with the rest of the staff or drawing strength from their physical presence but they made an interested audience as he explained his own presence. Then he made his way, oboe case in hand, to the hall. The band was presumably to eat after its labours. Mitchell followed strains which he could only hope were tuning-up noises and found the band, about forty strong and well disciplined, busy on the platform.

Mr Chandler, tapping on his music stand to gather their attention, had evidently been as unyielding as Annette had anticipated. Tim sat on a chair in the body of the hall, just below the stage, his shoulders hunched in an attitude that betokened a recent chastening. Mitchell walked over to the boy who caught sight of the case in his hand and leapt to his feet in delight. However, the band had begun its first piece and Tim knew better than to interrupt it. The noise was competent and considerable. Under cover of it, Mitchell administered his own rebuke on Hunter's behalf.

'You've wasted half an hour of my valuable time, Timothy, and I assure you I did it out of consideration for Inspector Browne, not sympathy for you. And I hear,' he went on, suddenly remembering the Inspector's account of his conversation with Valerie Kelsey the day before, 'you were in trouble for silly behaviour last time you were in this hall.'

Tim's face expressed astonishment at such omniscience, then amusement as he remembered the occasion. 'We were laughing,' he told Mitchell, 'at the Inspector's namesake, his and dad's.' He brought out the noun with a slight emphasis. It was obviously a new acquisition to his vocabulary.

Mitchell was impressed that an eleven-year-old was familiar with even the name of Sir Thomas Browne. He'd looked it up himself when he'd heard Hunter make learned allusions to it. How could he reveal his ignorance of a famous, or even an infamous, Jeremy Hunter?

'I was only saying,' Tim went on, aggrievedly, 'that Inspector Browne and Dad work very well together, not against each other all the time like them.'

Mitchell decided to come clean. 'Who are you talking about?'

Tim's tone indicated his scorn for such slow-wittedness. 'Tom and Jerry. They were on the cartoon programme on telly on Tuesday.'

Mitchell let this sink in as Tim chatted on. 'Then we were giggling at old Pa Frayn. He wasn't singing the wrong tune like he usually does, but, when we looked round at him, he'd got his gown all caught up behind him. It was way up above his knees like a black ballet frock. And then, when the hymn was over and we were nearly bursting with trying not to laugh, Mr Maynard said my word.'

Mitchell was mystified. 'Your word?'

Tim explained. 'We have games we play, because assemblies are so boring. In RE Mr Brook taught us how to use a concordance. Then, Briggsy in our form thought of another use for it. There's a long Bible reading in every assembly, so we all chose two numbers, one for

179

the page of the concordance and one for the word on it and we all have a word. During the reading, if your word's mentioned you get two points and we add them up each week.'

'What happens when you get the most?'

Tim shrugged. 'Nothing, really. It's just something to make the reading go quicker. My word is "praise" and Mr Maynard was reading a psalm that said, "The dead do not praise the Lord." I thought afterwards that it fitted in pretty well, seeing as Miss Bland couldn't come and read the lesson and prayers because she'd had her head bashed in, but, of course, none of us knew that then.'

A breathless small girl suddenly shot into the hall and collapsed, panting, on the floor beside them. She scrabbled frenziedly with the catches on her flute case, then took the three sections of the instrument out with more care and quickly fitted them together with the ease of long practice. Satisfied that it was properly assembled, she blew gently into the mouthpiece to warm it before glancing at Tim.

'Is he in a bad mood?' she asked fearfully.

Tim shrugged. 'He is with me!' He turned back to Mitchell. 'Lucy was laughing in Wednesday's assembly as well, but no one made her stand at the front. She shouldn't have been in the hall, either. Why were you?' He turned to her accusingly.

Her gesture indicated the unaccountability of teachers. 'Mrs Rivers didn't want me.'

Mitchell asked quickly, 'Didn't want you for what?'

The look on her face enquired what business it was of his but she replied politely enough. 'It was my turn to go to the domestic science room after registration to put all the used tea-cloths and things from the day before in the washing machine. But Mrs Rivers stopped me on the corridor and said she'd be in there herself and she'd see to the washing. I said I could do it without disturbing her and she was dead narky. She always is if you don't do just what she says without arguing.'

The blaring noise suddenly stopped and Mr Chandler

turned in the silence to the two miscreant members of his band. 'If you two feel quite ready to join us . . . ' They slipped, as unobtrusively as possible, into their places whilst Chandler thanked Mitchell for the assistance he had rendered. As he raised his baton to resume the practice, Mitchell left the hall, trying to repress his mounting excitement. He hurried through the foyer into the car park and used his radio to contact Inspector Browne. Keeping his voice steady and his message brief, he related his conversation with the two children. Two minutes later, much gratified by both the Inspector's approbation and his instructions, he re-entered the school. This time he met Maynard in the foyer and asked permission to wait there, sheltered from the wind, until the Inspector picked him up.

For five minutes he parried the anxious interrogation of the acting head until Browne's car appeared in the drive, whereupon Maynard accompanied Mitchell to meet it and to question the Inspector. 'Do you think we're rash to go ahead as normal, to reopen the school?' Maynard asked without preliminaries.

'It depends what you mean.' Browne wound the front passenger window further down whilst Mitchell shrugged and climbed into the back seat. 'If you're asking for a guarantee that everyone in the building is safe, I can't give it. But neither would you all necessarily be safe if you stayed at home. It depends whether our killer has a grudge against anyone else. How are things going, anyway?'

Maynard sighed. 'We're somewhat depleted. It was only to be expected, of course, but, because of the small numbers, the staff are depressed and resentful. They know we're just showing the flag rather than getting useful work done. There was unanimous support for the concert to go ahead. Surprisingly, only Kevin thought it would be disrespectful. They want me to impose a three-line whip on the parents from Monday, measures taken against absentees who aren't ill. I don't think it's wise, personally. I suppose, Inspector, you've no idea how long it might be before an arrest can be made?'

'I can't tell you,' Browne answered, carefully and thoughtfully. 'Any news of Miss Stafford, by the way? She's still in hospital, I take it?'

Maynard managed a smile. 'Yes to both your questions. They'll send her home today. They don't think she ever intended to kill herself. Actually, that's a big problem off our shoulders. Julian went to visit her during his two free periods this morning.' His smile widened. 'He does actually have some lessons to teach. He just happens to have his free time on Wednesday and Friday mornings. He had a useful chat with her and she's decided to resign. Neither I nor Sarah could persuade her to do it. It's possible that, because he had no official right to advise her, she was prepared to listen to him.'

He turned and gazed at the rising hillside. 'Julian would make an able successor to Sarah. He's a bit long in the tooth, maybe, for a first headship, but he'd have time to get the place back on its feet again before he retired.'

Browne looked at him, small, intense, worriedly seeking what was best for the school. 'I don't think you're doing a bad job yourself,' he countered. 'I've noticed how anxious everyone is to co-operate with you. There's more than one kind of charm, you know.'

Warmed himself by Maynard's delighted smile at this unexpected compliment, Browne drove away. Mitchell's conversation with the two youngsters had suggested two new lines of investigation and he needed the co-operation of the SOCO boys again.

Back in his office, with Mitchell unwillingly despatched to more mundane duties, he managed to contact Donaldson, make his explanation and put his two requests. 'Yes, the outlet drains to all the washing machines. Let's hope they haven't been used today. Do it as discreetly as possible. Can Swann do the other place? Tell him to use the back door. I don't want him seen and anybody warned. I'm not sure exactly what he's to look for. I've put you in the picture. Just do a more thorough search than I did last time.'

Satisfied that they would do their best for him, Browne

returned to the routine work on his desk and tried to close his mind to the case. He was soon disturbed by Hunter, coming to report on his morning's discoveries.

Comfortably astride the chair, Hunter reviewed Rivers's alibi concisely. 'It's a bit vague but everything he gave to Mitchell checks out, sir. His wife saw him at eight twenty-five when she went back into the house for something she'd forgotten. He was at the telephone, trying to get Miss Bland. No one saw him leave for his appointment at nine o'clock. That means nothing. With the drive emerging to the road out of sight of other houses, it's unlikely anyone would. He was early for his meeting in Leeds at nine forty-five. It's more significant that nobody noticed the car in the neighbourhood of the school. There aren't so many Mercs cruising about in that area. No one noticed any car that doesn't do its routine journey every morning. A couple of hangers-about described to the house-to-house squad could be him but the accounts are all so vague that there's nothing we can pin to him.'

Browne nodded. 'And it's very unlikely that he got into the grounds, let alone the building, without being seen by someone who'd recognise him.'

'That's right, sir. Besides, if he'd wanted to get rid of Miss Bland, she'd have been only too willing to arrange to meet him and then he could have despatched her unobserved. If we're fishing in the right pool, the lady seems the more likely catch.' Duty done, Hunter felt it was Browne's turn to divulge. 'I hear you've been visiting, sir.'

Browne recounted the morning's progress and they waited together for the telephone call from the lab, filling the time by attending to the contents of a wire tray. The thundercloud on Hunter's brow told Browne that the temporary truce between his sergeant and his brightest constable was over. The fact that Mitchell's opportunity to assist the investigation was a result of his son's irresponsibility and his wife's connivance at it was salt in Hunter's wound. Yet, in spite of the stormy atmosphere, another hour of useful paperwork had been done when the telephone shrilled and Browne reached for the receiver.

Hunter waited impatiently, making what he could of Browne's quiet 'Good work . . . You're sure of that? . . . That's a bonus. Thanks a lot for being so prompt.' The Inspector rang off and stood up. He offered no explanation but his face told Hunter that the case was solved.

'School finishes at five to four, doesn't it? Fix a car and be outside in it as soon as you can. I'll explain as much as there's time for whilst you drive.' As they set off, he did.

'Drive past the main entrance,' he instructed as they reached the school, 'and park on the road. We'll walk across the pitches. Not many windows give on to them and we've a good chance of getting to the head's office unobserved – the way White went on Wednesday. I want this done very carefully. I don't want the papers tonight full of stories about child hostages. We'll see Maynard and take his advice on how to take charge of this customer.'

As far as they could judge, the two policemen managed to reach Maynard's room unnoticed by even Mrs Weston who was incarcerated once more in the duplicating room, creating a clamour that masked their entry. Maynard could see from their faces that they were on serious business and listened as Browne briefly explained the purpose of their visit and the need for his advice. He blenched but when he spoke he was philosophic enough.

'Well, Inspector, it had to be one of us. Whichever one you had named the others would have felt disbelief and shock. If you'll tell me what you, and possibly I, have to do now, we can get it over.'

Browne told him.

He nodded and thought for a minute. 'It's room five you want. I think, if you don't mind, I'd better come with you. I'll go in and say you want a word and offer to stay with the class for a few minutes. I agree that if you go in we might have a child grabbed for bargaining with and we can't just send a message. No teacher here would leave a class unattended and they would all smell a rat if I asked them to do it.'

He reached for his gown, thinking aloud as they set off. 'I'll call the school together when you've finished your business and make an announcement. It's better that they all hear the truth from me than get their information from rumours and inaccurate press reports. Are you going to make a formal arrest now?'

With an affirmative nod, Browne passed through the fire doors into the main corridor, and looked with interest at the school in session. The classrooms had low windows giving on to the corridor and affording to passers-by a clear view of the proceedings within. Most teachers had protected themselves by fixing to the glass a variety of posters, magazine cuttings and specimen's of pupils' work and a tantalizing back view of these confronted the trio.

In the room labelled eight, all was noise and chaos. Only half the pupils were seated; the rest milled about, ignoring the young master whose expression of anxious pleading belied his shouted threats. Browne glanced at Maynard who displayed neither shame for, nor indignation at, the disorder. He was completely preoccupied with trying to steel himself for the ordeal ahead and unaware of the rowdiness of the class. They, however, suddenly became aware of him and his companions. The ringleader abruptly leapt from the desk where he had been standing to conduct the proceedings, in an attempt to lose himself amongst his followers. An unexpected silence fell and the master, highly embarrassed, was left bellowing into it.

The next room was unoccupied. Browne wondered if, even in these days of overcrowded schools, the teacher timetabled into it had preferred an empty store cupboard or unoccupied corner of the playground to competing with the din from next door. On the blackboard, under a map, skilfully executed in coloured chalk, someone had written 'Please Leave.' Browne chuckled at a fancy that the class for whom it was intended had interpreted this as a request to themselves with which they had obligingly complied.

In room six an elderly lady dictated into a quiet broken only by the scratching of pens and heavy sighs. Browne smiled to himself again. Here was the sort of education parents understood. When their offspring were thus occupied and brought home fat notebooks bursting with information, they knew they were getting good value for the taxes they paid. Miss Smithson thought they were too. Their homework essay was up on the board. 'James the First, The Wisest Fool in Christendom. Discuss.' Miss Smithson's class was doing proper history, not all this nonsense Miss Stafford wanted to introduce about politics and the modern world! The voice droned on, ink flowed and wrists and fingers ached. Browne guessed their minds were far away from the subject; probably their teacher's was, too.

They had arrived. The three men focused their attention on room five. As the teacher's voice paused, a ripple of amusement passed over the class. It was interrupted by a further remark, whereupon the ripple became a great wave of laughter that broke against the classroom walls. A hand was lifted, palm towards the class and instantly there was expectant silence. A question followed. After several seconds' pause whilst the class considered it, a forest of hands. The questioner gave reciprocal polite consideration to an unexpected answer.

His face still frozen and expressionless, Maynard muttered, 'What a waste,' and moved forward to enter the room. Standing well back, Browne and Hunter heard Maynard's mutterings, followed by his subordinate's polite explanation to the class that, since the Inspector wished to ask a few more questions, their lesson had, temporarily, to be interrupted. A suitable piece of work was suggested for Mr Maynard to supervise, then the room's former occupant emerged and, seeing the Inspector, offered his hand.

Sadly, Browne shook his head and instead of returning the greeting, made the formal charge. 'Julian Frayn, I arrest you . . .'

Two rooms further along the corridor, a door opened and Valerie Kelsey came out. After one glance at their grasp, one officer on each of Frayn's arms, she recognised the facts of the situation. Her face crumpling, she dived across the corridor and out through the foyer. Browne hoped that she wouldn't realise her own degree of involvement or blame herself. Then he knew that the hope was both vain and unnecessary. Frayn read his thoughts and consoled him.

'She had to know. She'll get over it. Perhaps, in time, she'll write to me wherever I'm incarcerated and let me know I acted to some purpose.'

At opening time, Browne went to the Owl and sat in the alcove opposite Draper's picture. After a search, Hunter found him there. He too stared at the picture, then at his chief. 'I'm not sharing this alcove again with that malevolent-looking creature,' he declared, moving over to the fire and settling on the comfortably upholstered bench beside it. Browne picked up his glass and followed and they toasted their feet. The evening was sunny but chilly and the fire was cheerful.

Hunter drank deeply before he spoke. 'You had your eye on Frayn right from the start.' It was half question, half statement.

'In my own speculations I concentrated on him but I investigated fully everyone else.'

'Just because he went home and showered? Miss Stafford went home as well.'

'I considered that pretty overwhelming evidence, but no, not just that. The more I talked to all the suspects, the more he seemed to be the unbalanced one. The others all talked to me. Frayn projected an image, played word games.'

'But what did he get out of it? Where's his motive?'

'He thinks he had to destroy a woman who used her power to restrict the lives of talented young people.'

'He just thinks the nurture of academic ability is of supreme importance?' Hunter put his glass down as a measure of his astonishment. 'But that's absurd. Was he going to put down every head he worked for who mentioned the rough with the smooth in school references? Or did he have some sort of relationship with that particular girl?'

187

Brown considered. 'I don't think there was anything improper in that sense, no sexual element. It's not as simple as that. He was frustrated, but not sexually. It was fatherhood that he was deprived of. I told you his only child and its mother died before it was born. Then he got this bug that sterilised him. Perhaps he picked a second wife so much younger than himself so that he could father her – when he wasn't busy enjoying the privileges of a husband, of course. He's extremely intelligent. I think whenever he met very able children, ones he thought he might have fathered, he became obsessed with them and set himself to champion them to the last extreme. Apparently, Kate was very much against adoption, afraid of nurturing incompatible genes or something. I'm not sure whether he'd have made a good father when it came to the nitty gritty and the child failed to live up to his expectations in some way.'

'But you didn't convict him on airy-fairy evidence like that?'

'No. There were all sorts of pointers. Maynard suggested that he was taking an unreasonable attitude to this reference. Then several people said that he'd behaved in a manner abnormal for him in assembly on Wednesday, arriving late, not taking a hymn book, not singing the tenor line and altogether keeping an unusually low profile.

'Then, this morning, young Tim was telling Mitchell that he'd been reprimanded in that assembly for sniggering.' The thundercloud returned to Hunter's face. Browne ignored it. 'The big joke was that he thought Frayn's gown was caught up at the back. He said it looked like a black ballet frock on him. It seemed unlikely that the heavy folds of a gown shouldn't free themselves by their own weight if anything disarranged them. We had reasoned that the killer covered his stained clothing with Miss Bland's gown so it seemed likely that Frayn was wearing that one, which wouldn't reach to his knees. I needed some tangible evidence of it and the likeliest place seemed to be Frayn's bathroom where the clothes had been removed. We got no joy from the linen basket which was empty but Swann noticed that the panel that boxed in the bath had one corner newly pinned with bright steel tacks. When he asked Kate Frayn about it she proudly announced that she'd effected the repair herself when she noticed yesterday that it had come adrift. She was put about when Swann ripped it off again. We were in luck. Frayn had rammed his soiled shirt and the gown behind it before he washed. We picked up a thread from the gown from a rusty nail projecting through to the underside of the panel and a minute smear of blood on the outer side of the bath matches Miss Bland's. That was very lucky considering the small amount of splattering there must have been on the shirt.

'Incidentally, Tim's little flute-playing friend complained that she'd been turned away from her usual Wednesday job of helping Mrs Rivers wash the tea-cloths. Mrs Rivers was doing the washing herself on Wednesday, thank you very much, so, just to be sure, I had Donaldson taking samples from the drainage pipes.'

Browne rested his voice whilst he refilled their glasses. When he came back Hunter asked, 'How has Frayn's wife taken it?'

'Phlegmatically, from what I can gather. Frayn wanted to phone her and when we allowed him to he calmly gave her various commissions concerning different members of the sixth-form and, apparently with equal calm, she undertook them. He told me he had no grudge against the police and, apart from worrying about Kate, no remorse.'

They finished their drinks in silence.

Frances Maynard sat beside her husband on a wooden bench in front of the lawns which bordered the open market. She was regretting his decision to let this concert for the Saturday shoppers go ahead. It was not because the curious crowds had turned out to listen more to the children's gossip than their virtuosity on various brass and woodwind instruments but because of the biting wind which penetrated her thick tweed coat and chilled her to the bone. However, Joanna's blue hands in their fingerless half gloves seemed to be darting nimbly enough over the flute keys and Virginia Browne's purple ones managed the valves of her French horn with equal dexterity. Their lips in their pinched faces looked too stiff to blow, but with their bright eyes fixed on Barry Chandler, who, for their entertainment, pranced and cavorted, baton in hand, perilously near the edge of the bandstand, they produced music that was cheerful and competent. She supposed they were used to the cold.

Mercifully, they were nearing the end of their programme. Frances let her eyes wander over the busy shoppers, the gay awnings and the fascinating variety of merchandise and savoured the mouth-watering smell from the hot dog stall a few yards away.

A loud drum roll and a sudden clash of cymbals caused panic amongst the pigeons at her feet. The old lady feeding them from a plastic bag glared at Chandler's unheeding back, whilst the sparrows, smaller but more stout-hearted, continued feeding.

In the uproar, Frances poked her husband to attract his attention. 'You wait for Joanna,' she mouthed. 'I'm going to see Kate.'

Maynard looked surprised. 'She's got her mother with her.'

'That's no use.' Frances was already moving away. 'Her mother never wanted her to marry Julian.'

Maynard put an arm out to stop her. 'Let Kate cope in her own way and her own time. She knows where we are.'

Frances sat down again, unwillingly, envying Chandler his excuse to exercise vigorously and keep warm. Presently, she felt her husband's hand on her arm in what she thought was a conciliatory gesture, but when she looked up he was nodding his head towards the market entrance.

Through it, and along the path towards them, came Kate Frayn, her head held high. They nodded in acknowledgment of one another and Kate joined the group of children's parents at the foot of the bandstand. The instruments produced their final cadence. The parents, shoppers and Kate politely applauded the band's performance. The Maynards rose to applaud Kate Frayn's.

From the flagged path, arriving to collect Virginia, Browne surveyed the group. Maynard was beginning a new career; so, in a way, were Kate and Julian Frayn. For the moment, though, his own job was done. About to bundle the French horn into the back of his car and his daughter into the front, he saw that he had been anticipated by young Mitchell. Smiling to himself, he drove home for lunch.